Strive for Life
Based on a True Story

Strive for Life

Based on a True Story

Murra Kenneford
with
Kathy Alba

Wichita KS

Strive for Life

Based on a True Story

All rights reserved. © 2006 by Murra Kenneford with Kathy Alba

No part of this book may be reproduced or transmitted by any form or by any means, graphic, electronic, or mechanical, including photocopying, recording, taping, or by any information storage or retrieval system, without the permission in writing from the publisher.

ISBN: 0-9709909-5-2

Printed in the United States of America by Signature Book Printing, Inc. www.sbpbooks.com

Thatch Tree Publications, Wichita KS

Text, cover, and page design by Kathy Alba, Ph.D.

For information:

> Thatch Tree Publications
> 2250 N. Rock Road, Suite 118-169
> Wichita Ks 67226
> email: ThatchTreePub@aol.com

Other titles by Kathy Alba, Ph.D.
> Speaking and Writing Good Well:
>> Empowering Yourself with "Proper" English:
>> Your Dynamite Guide to Conquering the World
> Concertos in D Major, A Novel
> Across the Soul's Boundary, An Epic in Seven Volumes
>> Volume One: Lifekeys

Dedicated to
Dr. R. Lemon
for his devoted
medical care

Best Wishes
Vera

Maura K
(Ekman)

In loving memory of
Bonnie Kenneford
1950 - 2003

Introduction

Once upon a time in a place far, far away. . . . Hmmm. Once you've read those words, your expectations no doubt light into fantasy: you may imagine a hunky prince tying up his alabaster-white steed to a rose bush and sweeping into the castle to plant the-kiss-that-will-change-everything on the lips of the slumbering princess. Pretty soon you anticipate that the couple will jump right into living happily ever after, and you'll be content to set down the book with a feeling that all is right with the world while you stir together some Helper with that hamburger from the freezer for dinner. As little girls, we grow up with a vague sense that life is *supposed to be* like this, that anything less is somehow unfair, even wrong. And maybe a deeply-seated trust in the fairytale complexion of life sets us up for an extra measure of disappointment when genuine reality finally burns into our skin. But even still, even as blistered as we may become, we still try to hold onto the dream.

In other words, once upon a time in a place not all that far away a precious and perfect child was born and welcomed into the world by an adoring extended family. Dimpled and plump with the softness of babyhood, she reminded everyone of the downy cherubs adorning the ceilings of baroque French palaces. They called her Bonnie to celebrate her "bonny-ness" or sweet and pure, even angelic, qualities. But within six months of the glorious event, the father removed himself from all the loving and doting on Bonnie then in progress as well as the trust of two sons and a young wife. He withdrew all his support for them, both physical and financial. In a big way, it was reality's fire kindled right from the beginning.

Devastated, the mother—actually, I'm the one sharing Bonnie's experiences with you—asked her own parents to care for the child until the home situation could be improved. For this reason, Bonnie thrived with farm life to the age of six among the potato and wheat crops and the Canadian cattle pastures near Calgary, Alberta. Finally, at that time in her young life Bonnie was able to rejoin our little family. And after several more years, I remarried; and we moved to southern California.

So had the fairytale life most of us grow up expecting been restored? Yes, apparently so. Bonnie graduated happily from a Los Angeles high school and then from college with a teaching degree and finally launched a career (a cheerful change of mind, however, into a medical environment) in the health care system.

She blossomed into a lively, energetic, highly capable individual, eventually a member of middle management in her company. She had the dedication and friendship of her employees, a lovely home, a devoted mother. All was well.

Or was it?

Is it ever?

By no means a fairytale, this is a story about Bonnie's reality—an account of how she clung to the dream while struggling to conquer potential tragedy.

Chapter One

1996

The shower's hot spray felt invigorating on that exquisite spring morning. Sun from the skylight overhead dappled the wet drops on the tiles like dew on pale lilies, and Bonnie sensed that the movements of such a morning could only lead to a one-of-a-kind, even profound sort of day. She shut off the water and reached for a towel, smiling to herself. *Joie de vivre,* the French called it: joy of living. Bonnie sighed a deep one filled with contentment.

But as she patted herself dry, one particular moment seemed to stop dead and pull together as if trying to form itself into marble—a monument to memorialize the event. She had discovered a lump in her breast. As with seemingly countless other women of this generation before her, the adrenaline of a lifetime splashed through her body as the realization struck home: *"Cancer?"* her mind pounded. *"No way. I'm only 46 years old!—a young person with all this terrific living to do! This is not happening!"* Hardly noticing, she finished drying herself and pulled on some clothes—tasteful ones even in the throes of a crisis—and leapt for the phone. *"So is our family history of the disease finally about to claim me too? This isn't possible; I've never been sick, and I feel just great."*

After dialing the first of two friends she

had in mind, Bonnie shut her eyes to blank away the singe of too much reality and waited for a voice to replace the ring tone.

"Shirlyn? It's Bonnie. Isn't it just the most gorgeous day?"

Laughing, "When *isn't* it a gorgeous one there around Palm Springs! We have a gag's worth of smog here thank-you-very-much. What's up?"

"Oh, nothing much really. I was sort of wondering if you remember the name of the doctor there in LA who did that biopsy on the gal across the street from you. Something oriental, I think?"

"Good grief—*why!*"

"Well, I sort of found a lump—you know, the smallest one you could ever imagine. Not much of a big deal; I'm sure it's totally nothing. But do you remember the name?"

"Um . . . Whang. I'm pretty sure it's Whang. Let me see if I can find him in the phone book. Hold on a second." A light twitter of pages. "Yes, here it is. Beverly Hills. The guy must be wonderful judging from the fancy address. His number is area code 310, 555-8346."

"Great, I'm sure he'll be fine. I know it couldn't be anything serious, but I thought I may as well get it checked. I'll let you know when the appointment is, and we'll have to do lunch— something extravagant and filled with calories, preferably chocolate ones!"

"You bet! Bring it on! That sounds terrific, Bonnie. It's been much too long."

At last Bonnie set down the phone on the dresser and paused to sniff at a glorious arrangement of daffodils and baby's breath she had set there to celebrate the fragrance and promise of new spring. And after she had padded to the kitchen for a few tight swallows of water, she returned to dial the Los Angeles oncologist's number.

The waiting room, drowsing a faintly eastern mood of cool jade and dove gray, tried to swaddle Bonnie in its comfort against the agony normally felt by participants in this often-repeated scene. Still, Bonnie had little need for such consoling because she knew this cancer test thing would prove negative, that she would soon get back to the rest of her life of laughter and kindness and helping with the health of others. Without delay, she reached for a copy of *People* magazine—for she always enjoyed following the fortunes and wardrobes of celebrities and wannabe stars—and settled down to remember what spangles each of the nominees had worn to the Oscars last month when *The English Patient* had swept up the Best Picture award.

At last, a nurse slipped into the main room from a dim hallway beyond and glanced around. "Bonnie Kenneford?" She pushed her glasses higher on her nose and nodded when this next of her patients rose and began to come forward. "How are you feeling, Ms. Kenneford?"

"Oh—I feel wonderful! I'm not even sure why I'm here because I know there's nothing wrong with me—I never get sick. At this point I'm not even positive I felt a lump at all, but of course it never hurts to make sure."

Smiling, "I wish everyone who comes

13

through this office had your sense of good timing and courage." She ushered Bonnie into an examining room.

"Well, it just makes sense to take care of things." Quickly Bonnie's eyes darted here and there about the space, an automatic necessity. "What elegant prints!" she exclaimed at the pastel watercolors of ballerina-like figures along the shore. "Your decorator has amazing taste."

"Yes, she certainly does. Actually, it's Dr. Whang's wife who has the fun of choosing all the art work and design features around here." Pausing to reach for some equipment, "Why don't you sit up here, and I'll get your blood pressure."

Bonnie scooted up on the table and stared into the pale tints of the softly washed ocean while the cuff squeezed her arm several times. "How am I doing?"

"It's 85 over 130."

"Whoa, that's really high for me!"

"Everyone who comes in here seems to say the same thing—anxiety, hon, you know? It's completely normal."

"Well, that's odd because I mostly feel *calm*. Somehow my emotions must've had trouble communicating that to the beat of my heart."

"Either way, I'm sure you'll do great. Here's a gown you can put on—let's see—why don't you go ahead and have it open in the front."

Bonnie grasped the wad of gauzy blue with its multitude of string ties. "Oooo—totally charming!"

14

Grinning, "Yeah, you bet—right off the Christian Dior runway!" The nurse straightened several particulars on the counter. "Doctor will be in to chat with you in a few minutes; he shouldn't be long."

"Oh, thanks, no problem. I'll be fine."

Now alone, Bonnie sat in the stillness and pulled in a long breath. What could she say in the face of the unthinkable? What can any of us say? Her musing mind set up a sort of mantra: *"I'll be fine. I'm sure of it. I know I'll be just fine."*

Dr. Whang had asked her to lie down while he performed a preliminary inspection of the lump.

"Yes," he said, scowling and prodding at the area in question, "I must biopsy this right away."

Hesitating in the force of his negativity, "Have I come in too late?"

"I was told you came here as soon as you discovered the lump?"

"Yes, immediately."

"Well, I can't answer that—whether you're too late or not; I'll know more after we examine some tissue." He straightened abruptly with a sniff. "As the nurse must have explained, I'll be doing that in our operating room here during this hour. The nurse will help you get ready; but to give you some idea of what to expect, you'll be placed under some anesthetic—less than a general but more than a local."

"I'll be unconscious but able to breathe on my own, no machinery?"

"That's right. I shall only take a few minutes for the procedure. I should have the results back in a few days—sometime about the middle of next week." His hand was on the doorknob, but the eminent man seemed to remind himself, "Do you have any questions?"

"Will there be pain from the biopsy?"

"Not really," he smirked, apparently put off by her pettiness. "But if you *do* find yourself with discomfort, I'll allow some meds to help you *cope.*" He now had the door opened.

"What about complications?"

His expression seemed almost offended. "This is just a simple little procedure, madam! I do thousands of these every week. Hundreds of thousands."

Bonnie had no trouble mustering a bit of her habitual spunk. "I'm terribly sorry to be taking up so much of your time."

Realizing he had been wearing his super-surgeon's face too transparently, he offered a controlled smile and as much of an apology as he could afford. "No problem! That's what I'm here for."

The next few days had stretched endlessly. Waiting for the results of a biopsy yanks the smooth ribbon of time into ugly shreds for anyone alive, but Bonnie had been suffering even more from a sudden, inexplicable pain in the breast that the doctor had examined. She believed she could have managed the suspense and dread of not knowing almost gracefully, but she had no reasonable way to account for the almost intolerable heaviness that had been growing during this anxious time.

16

In fact, by Wednesday she had needed to stay home from work, a relatively new experience in her career. Lounging in the curving living room couch, she let her vision wander across the ambience of white tile to the palm tree grove out the front window, seeing little of the scene. *"Shall I put more ice packs on this pain? What an old toad I am—sitting around here like this! Even a bra gives basically zero support for this sack of beans. So do I really have cancer, and not only that but the tumor has grown to the size of an orange overnight? How does a person fight something like this? It's driving me crazy."*

Actually, Bonnie had become so distracted wondering about the striking condition that she startled almost out of her chair when the cell phone began crooning her favorite, "Love me tender, love me true, never let me . . ."

"Hello? Yes, this is she."

"Hi. I'm with Dr. Whang's office, Ms. Kenneford. I'm calling to report that the results of your biopsy revealed a malignancy and to schedule you for either a mastectomy or a lumpectomy, whichever seems appropriate after the doctor examines you further. Do you have any questions?"

Bonnie's mind raced. *"Any questions?! Is she kidding? 'You have cancer/have a nice day.' Is this how the modern age thumps down life-shattering news on a person's shuddering eardrums?"* But pulling her thoughts together, she managed to say, "Okay, I understand, but I have a serious problem in that breast that needs attention right away, yesterday." Explaining her situation with rapid-spilling words, Bonnie emptied her concerns; and the nurse reacted instantly.

Evening, the most red-gold wildfire of a sunset Bonnie could ever remember. She watched from the balcony of her Santa Monica hotel—one set on a grand but heavily eroding cliff—as the fiery disk seemed to pause for a last glimpse of the day and then slid languidly into a slot at the back of the ocean. Her skin ruffled with a chill, but it might have stemmed more from her mind than the growing darkness.

"Okay," she told herself, rubbing her upper arms, *"it's time for things to start going* right *with this week of my life; this has been just too weird."* Absently her sight lapped at the hectic lights popping on all around the bay and the length of the pier as if seeking hope in their sure sparkle. *"Not to speak badly of anyone, but that doctor is an incompetent mole! How did the nurse explain the problem?—'So sorry, but it seems he cut something by mistake during the biopsy and that cup of blood he took out of your breast had pooled there during this past week. That's what you were thinking might be the tumor grown so large all of a sudden.' Good grief! How unbelievable is that!"*

Gazing skyward, Bonnie grasped for solace among the familiar stars. Gradually, the sharp outlines of Orion had pricked the blackness far off to her left overhead. *"Hmmm. Pretty, as ever. Majestic even. But no comfort there, not in the sky; it has to be in myself if I'm to have any at all. . . . So what shall I think about the surgery back at home with that new doctor to-*

18

morrow? Do I trust anyone to do it right after what I went through with their fixing Dr. Whammy's little 'mistake' this morning? I can battle the cancer for all I'm worth—and conquer it, of course; but can I trust any doctor at all to give me that fighting chance?" She pulled her sweater up closer around her throat against an onshore breeze just now stirring up. "Good question, and I wonder how much sleep I'm apt to get tonight, thinking about the procedure tomorrow and the new doctor I'm going to try. When will life seem real again?"

Chapter Two

1996

The trip from Los Angeles back to the Palm Springs area several hours east had happened almost out of Bonnie's awareness, so focused was she on the events of these days. She drove automatically with her mind elsewhere, little bothered by the insistently crawling freeway traffic that could ordinarily cause such annoyance.

Just now she had met her mother, Murra, in the lobby of the hospital near her home; and the two were checking in and preparing to wait for Bonnie to be called for the surgery.

"I'm glad you could be here, Mom," Bonnie began, gazing out at a lush azalea garden, ablaze with pink under tall swaying palms.

Patting her hand, "Well, sweetheart, this is exactly where I want and need to be. More than that, I wish I could do this for you, instead of you; I've had a chance to live, but you haven't—not anywhere near enough."

"But I'm *going* to live, Mom: I'll just dig right in and conquer this thing. You know how healthy I am—and strong. This isn't going to be that big a deal, at least if I can get a doctor that has a clue. I mean—look how many people get cancer and survive these days! If this were ten or fifteen—" Bonnie's pronouncements were cut off when a nurse signaled to her from a doorway across the room. "Oh, Mom—she's calling

20

me. You'll be here when I get through?"

"Absolutely, you can count on it."

"If you feel like praying, will you do that?"

"I've already started."

Once Bonnie had passed beyond the door, she found herself in a spacious room with several beds surrounded by privacy curtains (currently all opened), each with lockers as well as a scattering of medical equipment and monitors.

"This is an outpatient recovery room," she suggested to herself. *"It doesn't look as radically high tech and filled with hoopla as, say, a cardiac ICU or something. This won't be that bad."*

Breaking into her thoughts, the nurse gestured toward a locker. "You can put all your things in here, and this is the gown you'll be wearing for the surgery. And these cute booties!"

Laughing, "Ah—can't forget those! Can't get cut open without toasty toes. Thanks for helping me get ready."

"It's my pleasure. You'll be coming back here after the procedure for a little while until you're feeling well enough to get up and head out."

"How long will all this take?"

"It's hard to say; that is, Dr. Natarajan won't know how much needs to be done until he has a better idea of the extent of the cancer. But if you look on the bright side, it'll only *feel like* a few minutes. Once you go to sleep, the next thing you'll be aware of is waking up and finding everything finished. One hour or six: it would be all the same from your point of view."

"That really is a good way to think about it."

"Yes. And when you're fully awake, Dr. N.

will come back here and explain what he found and what he did to fix it."

Just then a slender man with a bushy moustache entered Bonnie's curtain area and extended his hand. "Hello, Ms. Kenneford? I'm Dr. Ronnebaugh your anesthesiologist. I'll be in charge of keeping you knocked out during the procedure. I'm wondering if you have any questions or problems you'd like to clear up before we start."

"Not really. . . . Well, I *have* heard that some people worry about being awake during their surgery and feeling every last thrust of the sword, so to speak, but not able to say anything—you know, to let the anesthesiologist understand the situation."

"Is that a particular concern of yours?"

"Not really, but I've heard that some people—"

Grinning, "It's never happened in my experience, and I'm going on 25 years as the gas man around here."

"Okay," she smiled in return, "then I'm bound to trust you."

"Good enough. Looks like we're ready to rock and roll."

"Eeee-haaw!"

The anesthesiologist strolled off toward the operating room next door to prepare his equipment, and the nurse helped Bonnie finish packing away her clothes in the locker and adjusting her gown.

At last Bonnie was shown into the area where everything was set up for the surgery. She climbed up onto the table and offered the room

22

a dry laugh. "A fascinating maze of stuff you've got here, doctor. What's next?"

"I'll get an IV going in your wrist here, and in a flash you'll get to start counting backwards from 100, no sweat. Think of it as a great little vacation from an otherwise stressful day. And immediately after that, Dr. Natarajan will commence his slicing and dicing. Just kidding."

"Gotcha!" And in a moment after she had watched the IV needle being arranged, she began, "One hundred, ninety-nine, ninety-eight, ninety-seven, ninety . . ."

"Oh my God! They've wakened me up too soon! I'm still in the operating room under all these lights! Is this crazy or what? I trusted him!" Bonnie felt activities engaging her chest and under her arm and heard low voices, and this sent a wave of fear shooting all through her limbs. But in fact, the surgery was finished, and the bandages and drainage tube in her breast were merely being adjusted. It was exactly the right time for her to be regaining consciousness, but with a pang she felt a little sorry.

At once she was rolled back to the recovery room. Her normally quick impressions were coming as if in slow motion while her vision limped against these blurring surfaces. Abruptly she began shivering violently, something she wasn't expecting.

"Now what!" she exclaimed to the nurse.

"Oh, it's just the effect of the anesthesia wearing off; it's normal for many patients. Here are a couple of blankets for you. This shouldn't last too long."

23

Actually, the shuddering kept on longer than she would have preferred, but eventually she was distracted away from it when Dr. Natarajan scurried up to her bedside. A small man of Indian descent, he seemed to effervesce in all directions at once.

"Miss Bonnie—you are feeling back to yourself, no?" he said, patting her hand with spirit.

Chuckling, "Not exactly!"

"But better than a few minutes ago?"

"Um, I don't know: I was growing kinda fond of being oblivious to everything."

"Ah yes! Well, my dear, I want to tell you about how the surgery went."

The color faded even further from her face but she managed a jaunty, "I'm all ears."

"It was splendid! Truly. I removed the tumor from your breast; then I took out a number of lymph nodes under the arm to be on the safe side."

"Do you think you got all the cancer?"

"Oh yes! I'm sure of it!" He bustled around the bed, adjusting the blankets and patting her foot.

Bonnie felt the purest relief she had ever imagined. "Way to go! So what happens next?"

"You'll come in for a series of six chemotherapy treatments, each one month apart; and those will be followed by six weeks of daily radiation. That will take up most of the rest of this year, but at the end of it you'll be just fine. Finer than fine!"

"It's just *so cool* to hear you say that! I'm excited to dig in and get this whole thing over

24

with."

"That's the spirit!"

Awhile later, Bonnie was feeling good enough to be dressed and moving around, so she strode out to the waiting room. As promised, her mother was present, sitting quietly with an expression of calm that a close faith in God can bring. She had prayed for a miracle; and from the way her daughter was smiling and strolling across the room, she suspected that wonder had been achieved in this hour.

"Hi tootsie," Bonnie exclaimed. "Are you ready to blow this place? Did you get through the waiting okay?"

"Well, my goodness, you look fabulous. Did you really have the surgery? I was expecting you—"

"Never mind about whatever you were expecting, Mom: Dr. Natarajan said he got all the cancer, and I'm here to tell you—I'm ready to take on the world. I'll drive home if you don't mind!" And so she did.

Chapter Three

1996

Warm, dry air soothing around the greenest and bushiest of palms and bright magenta bougainvillea blooms climbing a trellis covering one wall: the fine July evening offered itself as a reliable fill-in for paradise. Bonnie had always loved sitting here on the patio listening for the cricket concerto to rise as the sun slunk behind the Santa Rosa Mountains off to the west. But whereas she had once enjoyed serving margaritas and her own (easy) secret-recipe *chili con queso* to merry groups of friends here across the years, this summer had seen her staring at the same terra cotta tiles but from a chaise lounge and with the company of her mother alone. Putting her treasured career and its frequent necessities for travel on hold until she could gain back her strength, Bonnie had mostly been confined to her bed and this lounge chair since the surgery in April while she endured the special challenges of chemotherapy. She had told only two of her friends— Shirlyn in Los Angeles and Angelina here at home—and none of her acquaintances and business associates that she was being treated for cancer. No one must know.

The bark of a dog from a yard down the street broke into her meditation, another rehash of how annoying the idea of a drainage tube in her chest continued to be even after three months—half way through the six treatments.

26

"If this dopey catheter helps, it'll be worth the irritation; but I never imagined the pace of life to crawl so slowly. Seems like I would've had enough time to hopscotch around the equator five times with two lobes of my brain tied behind my back by now." Her gaze followed the flight of a bird in silhouette against the pale pink and gold tints growing across the sky. And as the wind chimes from the front porch lifted with the air, limply she reached for a sip of water but found the glass empty.

"Mom?" The call sounded hollow to her ears, but her mother was just coming outside from the kitchen. "Oh—there you are."

"Yes—hi, Bonnie. I've brought you some nice fruit salad and more ice water. Are you hungry?"

"Afraid not, but thanks. The water would be good though."

Murra set down the plate of mandarin oranges and grapes and refilled Bonnie's glass. The soft tinkle of ice against crystal seemed to soften the air. "Here's a cold pack for your headache too."

Smiling listlessly, "You're amazing, Mom. And here I'd always planned on taking care of you when you aged, not the other way around— and while I'm still young." She reached for the pack and laid it across her forehead, a place formerly flossing with short dark hair. Just touching the barren marble of her head caused a frown that seemed to stem up from the very bottom. "This is getting old, isn't it?"

"Half way through. . . ."

"Yeah. But Mom, what's going to happen

to me? Do you think all this nauseating chemo will really—"

"Let's just have faith; I'll keep praying that God will send us the rest of a miracle."

Softly, "You keep on doing that; it would be wonderful." She pulled the ice pack over her eyes. "But two of my friends who had cancer ended up *dying*. Angelina talks about them all the time."

"I know that. I remember. But that doesn't mean you—"

"But I've never been sick! I don't know how to *be* sick!"

With an attempt at a smile, "You're doing a very fine job of it." Murra shoved the little plate closer to her daughter. "Sure you couldn't manage a grape or two?" Adding a wink, "Maybe if I peeled them? Or I could—Bonnie? What is it! Bonnie?"

Abruptly Bonnie's hands and feet had begun twitching, an event startling enough that she could not hold back the tears. "Now what, Mom?" she gasped. "Now what? How will all this turn out?"

Murra scooted onto the lounge chair and held her only daughter and most precious friend. As the tremors eventually let down, she murmured, "Here, let me rub your back. Just turn there on your side, and maybe this will help you feel better." But would it? Could anything short of that miracle?

The next day, almost noon. Bonnie rolled over and squinted her eyes against the brightness pouring over her bed from the skylight above.

28

What had wakened her? Soft voices from the other room? Idly, her gaze wandered here and there among the pinks and blues of the room's southwest decor.

Just then Murra knocked gently and then entered with the care giver who stopped by weekly to see Bonnie. "Here's Leslie with your shot, Bonnie—nothing like the most cheerful way to wake you up!"

The nurse smiled, "Sorry about this."

Softly, "No, it's okay, Les. Anything you can give me to rev up the blood cells all this chemo is destroying is worth whatever it takes. See, it gets me strong enough to make it to the bathroom to barf rather than having to do it in my lap."

She laughed, "Well, missy, we aim to please!" With dispatch, she swabbed Bonnie's arm with alcohol and then proceeded with the injection. Pausing to take stock of the desperately ill woman before her, "Your color's better," she remarked, hoping her little fib might offer encouragement. "Have you been outside?"

Bonnie swallowed hard, realizing the nausea was working its way up and would soon demand movement out of this bed. Could she keep up the jaunty tone? "Yes, actually—yesterday in the late afternoon for a little while. Are you saying I'm sporting a gorgeous tan?"

"That just what I'm saying!"

"Great!—the world's first bald bathing beauty." Abruptly the theoretical tan drained from her face, and Bonnie threw back the light sheet and managed her own limp version of an explosion toward the bathroom. "Excuse me, people!"

Murra and the nurse exchanged glances while the sounds of vomiting scuffed from behind the closed door.

Whispering, "Has she been eating anything that stays down?"

"Very little, I'm afraid. And almost more than that, to be honest, I'm worried about her mood. She's never been sick, you see; and this experience has been pretty incredibly traumatic for her."

"It's traumatic for everybody, even those who are used to having illness, believe me. But she's becoming depressed—is that what you're saying?"

"Yes, absolutely. She tries not to let it show, but a mother can see these things."

Bending to reach for her bag, "Dr. Natarajan sent along some medication samples with me in case that happened. Have her take these following the dosage on the packet and see how she does; if the meds work, he'll call in a prescription for them."

"Wonderful. I'll let you know."

Early August. Gil Grissom and Catherine Willows had just discovered blood in a outlandish place; and the sample's DNA, of course, would clinch the case and send the "perp"—the one brutalizing the "vic" to death—to prison forevermore; another "CSI" was drawing to a close. Bonnie, lying in her usual station on the curving living room sofa, had figured out the guilty party early in the story; and now she was drowsing a bit while the plot pulled its complexities together

30

as she had foreseen. Murra watched her from the recliner beside the fireplace nearby, hardly paying attention to their favorite TV program—along with "Law and Order"—or the heavy scent of jasmine sighing through an opened window.

"She looks feverish and warm," Murra reflected. *"Wonder if there's anything I can do."* She paced across to feel her daughter's forehead. *"Mercy! She's on fire!"*

At the touch, Bonnie stirred with a small moan, then opened her eyes. "Mom? Oh—did I conk out on the ending of 'CSI'? Who's getting the axe?"

"I'm sorry; I guess I wasn't paying attention very well there at the end." Pausing, "You look like you have a fever; how do you feel? Can I get you anything?"

"I don't know, maybe some—" Abruptly Bonnie let out a small shriek and, backing up, jammed herself against one end of the couch. "Get them away, Mom! Do something!"

Adrenaline spurted her forward, "What is it!"

"Bugs! Big hairy ones! Crawling everywhere. Can you get them *off me?!*"

"Bonnie, I don't see any bugs. Are you sure?"

"MOM—do something!"

Murra huddled down beside her with arms all around. Softly she said, "I think it must be the medication. There aren't any real bugs in here."

"But I see them!" She collapsed her face against her mother's neck and wept.

"Then maybe try to keep your eyes closed.

They aren't really there." In a moment, "Let me get you some water and take your temperature. Something's just not right." As soon as Bonnie had calmed, still with her eyes shut against the fear, Murra rose to get the thermometer and stopped off to call the doctor.

When the temperature was recorded, she found it much too high. "Dr. Natarajan said to take you to the hospital under these conditions."

"No, Mom. I'm not going! My two friends who had cancer *died in the hospital.* I'm not getting anywhere near that place."

"But Bonnie, that isn't rational. The hospital didn't cause them to—"

"Never mind that!" she interrupted. "Just get me two aspirins and call Dr. Natarajan in the morning! End of discussion."

"We can give it a try. But Bonnie—"

"I'll be okay. I'm fighting this thing, don't you see?"

Sadly, from the very heart of her, "I see, honey. Yes, I see."

Chapter Four

1996

"Bonnie—isn't it exciting? Sometimes I've wondered how we'd get to this point because it was so rough, but here we actually are—the end of the chemo." Murra took a tentative sip of her tea and glanced across the table at her daughter.

"It feels wonderful, no kidding. Like a hippopotamus finally finding some water to buoy up his bulk and a nice rock for resting his chin."

"You mean, like being hit with a stick because it feels so good when you stop?"

Drily, "Yeah. Chemo has been one heck of a stick." Bonnie tried some of the tea as well. "But what do you suppose the next six weeks of radiation will be like? Worse?"

"Not much *could* be worse. But I know you'll get through it with all your usual grace."

Laughing, "Grace?" She cocked her head with the fingers of both hands pointing under her chin and batted her eyes as a living version of Betty Boop. "Who, me?"

"Yes, absolutely." Murra paused while she poured more tea for both of them. "What about after the six weeks are finished; have you given much thought to that? I know you've been planning to go back to work, but—would you mind if I make a small observation?"

"Of course not; I love hearing your opinions."

"Well, do you think you'll feel like doing so much traveling as before? You know how you would always be shooting off to all the different offices to fix things when the people there got themselves in trouble, but do you think your strength will—"

"As a matter of fact, Mom, I've been thinking about that very thing a *ton*. I loved every part of that job, but my thoughts are pretty much in a line with yours. That kind of pace, as hard as it is for me to admit it, seems like it would be a horrendous burden from my new, not-necessarily-improved, point of view."

"I'm thrilled to hear you say that. But what will you tell your boss?"

"Mac," she said, pressing her lips together in a sort of scowl. "That will be tough. Better get it over with ASAP, though, so I can start figuring out something else to do while I have these last weeks at home to think. And so he can be looking for someone to replace me." Bonnie gave her tea cup a small shove toward the center of the table. "In fact, maybe I'd better take care of it right now."

Rising, "Then I'll give you some privacy while you do." Murra handed her daughter the phone and cleared the tea set onto a tray that she carried into the kitchen.

"Hello, Mr. Gault's office."

"Lauren, this is Bonnie."

"Bonnie! How *are* you, kid? You've been on leave for so long I thought you might've fallen off the edge of the planet. Have you been to ev-

34

ery port in the orient, or what?"

"Mostly 'or what,' I'm afraid. Is Mac in? I need to speak with him."

"Oh, sure, hon; I'll ring him. . . . Great hearing from you. Hope to see you sooner than soon."

A pause, then Mac Gault's boom of a voice. "Bonnie! Holy Moses, am I ever glad to hear from you! When can you be here?—I'm assuming your leave is now to be over and you'll be back taking care of the place by this afternoon at least. You can't believe what chaos has ensued with all the temp people we've had in here. The company is about to fold."

"Well, Mac, that certainly is why I'm calling—that is, about my coming back to work."

"Thank God!"

"No," she paused for a breath deep enough to carry her inevitable negatives, "I'm afraid I'm not going to be able to fill my position any longer after all."

"What are you talking about!"

"It's the travel, Mac. I'd prefer not being gone that much or keeping up that kind of pace."

"What are you *saying*? You've *thrived* at that pace, young lady; you're as strong as twenty-six guys around here!"

Softly, "I'm afraid I have to disappoint you; the travel is just too much. I'm sorry."

"Sorry! This is perfectly unacceptable! You're the most capable person in this company; we simply can't do without your organizational acumen. As it is, the place is limping along waiting for you to come back and whip it into shape."

"I think you're exaggerating."

35

"Hell no! I can't accept your resignation, Bonnie, and that's final."

"I'm afraid you're going to have to."

"This is insane—the company will fold! It's already on the way there now!" He hesitated, then decided to use his big guns, no matter how insensitive. "What do you mean stringing me along like this all these months! If you were planning to wipe out on me, why didn't you just go ahead and do it six months ago? I call that unprofessional and—" he paused to come up with some additional words that he hoped would manipulate her guilt buttons, "—and irresponsible, and— and *dishonest*."

Bonnie felt the sting, no matter how unjustified. Of course she knew her lack of explanation was causing him anger rather than the compassion he might have offered had he understood her health situation, but she was determined not to parade her cancer before him like some pathetic plea for sympathy. No, he must never know. "I'm very sorry, Mac. That's all I can say."

"Well, hell! What kind of recommendation do you think you'll get from me for any future job you may try for? Huh? What do you think of that!"

Softly, "I'm afraid not much." She cleared her throat. "Again, I'm sorry for any inconvenience I'm causing, and—"

"INCONVENIENCE? Are you insane?"

"Goodbye, Mac. I'm sorry." And squeezing her eyes shut, Bonnie forced herself to hang up.

Murra leaned her face into the doorway. "That didn't sound like it went too well."

36

"Putting it mildly."

"What will you do now?"

Smiling, "Take two aspirins and call Dr. Natarajan in the morning! Something will work out; I'm sure of it."

Black cats and pumpkin cutouts in the windows were mocked by the bright dry sun when gloomy mists and damps seemed required at this time of year. Bonnie glimpsed at the seasonal decorations without really seeing them as she entered at the main doors of the Cancer Foundation of the Desert near Palm Springs. Dr. Natarajan's office was at the end of the hall on this first floor; and Bonnie headed directly there, car keys still in hand, without stopping to notice the room where all her chemo treatments had been given or the old-wicked-witch-on-broomstick effigies hanging in various doorways. How would these daily radiation events affect her life? Would she continue feeling so intensely ill as during the past six months? Bonnie walked into her doctor's office with hope along with misgivings.

Dr. Natarajan was buzzing around behind the reception bay when she stopped to check in. Animated in a bright white coat sharply contrasting with his dark skin, he was offering clipped observations along with general pats and well wishes to the staff members as well as assorted filing cabinets, piles of medical records, portable carts, and even the coffee machine as he fidgeted his way back to the treatment rooms along the hall.

"Ah Bonnie! How fine and splendid you

look! I'll be with you in—"

Just then one of the receptionists handed him a phone. "It's the AMA president on line one for you, doctor. About that lecture."

"I'll take it in my office," he fizzed, dashing from the room.

Smiling with resignation at Bonnie, the woman acknowledged, "You know how he is! Two hundred irons in twenty different fires all going at once. If you'll have a seat, I'm sure he won't be long . . . unless he has still another call, of course."

"Oh, this is perfect," Bonnie replied, picking up a copy of *Time Magazine*. "I'm behind on the gossip about JFK Jr.'s new bride and what Candidate Dole says about Candidate Clinton. And here's a nice article about that new movie, "The First Wives' Club"—the babes of which even made the cover," adding with a laugh, "Can I reschedule my appointment for late this afternoon so I can get caught up on all my heavy reading?"

"Gotcha!"

After a bit of a wait while the ever-in-demand oncology guru took several more calls (as Bonnie detected by over-hearing the receptionist), she was shown into a room to get started on this final phase of her therapy.

"Ah, Bonnie, Bonnie, Bonnie—" Dr. Natarajan cried as he darted through the opened doorway at last. "You're looking splendid!—pink and healthy, no?" With a swoop, he had pumped her hand, listened to her heart, and fussed himself into a chair which, however, he boiled out of just as quickly. "We will get your radiation

38

started at once, and then— Excuse me while I get rid of this page." Pausing, "Please call me this afternoon; I'm with an urgent patient right now." The man grinned as he clicked off the device. "You are urgent, no?"

"Completely."

"As I was saying, we'll get that radiation process over so you can get on with your life. You're planning to go back to work—is that what you told me?"

"Well, yes, I *was* planning to, but I'm afraid my former job required more traveling than I feel able to handle these days, so I'm currently not employed anywhere at all."

"Oh well! You shall come work for me here at The Foundation, of course. I have far, far too much to do, and for weeks I've been looking for someone with your perfectionistic organizational skills and—" he punctuated this with staccato nods of his head "your sense of humor!"

"What kind of job would it be?"

"Business Manager—that is, Director of Medicare, disbursements, etc. You will have eight persons working for you, and I know you will do a splendid job. Would you like to start as soon as the radiation is complete?"

Dazzled by his abruptness as much as his confidence in her, Bonnie drew in a deep breath and then laughed. "I guess that would be about as close to perfect as life can get! Thank you so very much, Dr. N."

"Splendid! Now let me get you started on the radiation, so you can hurry up and straighten out your new office!"

And immediately he did so that she could.

Chapter Five

1997—1999

The office was awash with brilliant slants of turquoise, green, and blue light, the afternoon sun sparkling through a stained glass panel—a tropical parrot among hibiscus blooms—set high amid the wall of glass that opened onto the front of the building. Bonnie's office always seemed to give off a sense of sunshine and the flowers of the heavenlies. Just now a tremendous display of birds of paradise graced a side table beside the coffee maker; and it was at this spot that she was standing, admiring the elaborate tinctures of light falling on her arms.

"This reminds me of my favorite Maui, an exotic carnival of colors, a festival for the eyes," she reflected. *"Definitely. But maybe if I keep standing here like this, the dizzy spell will pass and nobody will figure out about this brain blaster of a headache."* She remained motionless for another few seconds, apparently entranced with the elegance of the scene; but then, sensing movement into the room, she turned. "Beth! Come have some coffee with me. I've just made a new pot of the most scrumptious brew you've ever imagined. Please. Join me."

Bonnie's assistant had just entered with a stack of papers needing to be signed. "Do you have time?"

"For you? Always. Have a seat." Her hands

40

got busy with the coffee service. "A cookie? Fabulous chocolate chip? I'm afraid they're from the bakery—you know I can't cook, but at least my heart's in the right place."

"No thanks. I'd better not."

Bonnie came forward with a dainty china cup for her friend and set another on the outer edge of the desk for herself. At last she settled into the other of the two overstuffed chairs. "You look upset, kiddo. Has this afternoon been crummy to you?"

After a pause, "Oh, it's too petty to—"

"Nothing's too petty, Beth. I say if it's upsetting you, it's worth looking at. How can I help?"

The young woman gazed across at her boss, mentor, and friend. "Well, it's not about work, Bonnie."

"You know that's okay with me; you're important to me *apart from* work, Bethie." Smiling, "Got it?"

Beth grinned softly. "Got it." She paused for a sip of the coffee, a stall. "Um, Brad made some more comments about my weight last night. You know how I've been going to Weight Watchers and trying so hard to resist all the *cookies* that come my way in getting off all this post-baby weight, but he said I still look pudgy. Can you believe it?—*pudgy!*"

With a straight face, "The man should be shot. . . . Oh, wait—you need him to take care of Benny when you have to do errands or take a break from mommyhood once in awhile. Better keep him around."

Smiling in spite of herself, "Yeah, guess

41

I'd better. But what makes men say things like that?"

Still with a straight face, "Insensitive slobs."

Beth laughed, "You're right on that, Bonnie."

"What can I do to help?" The headache had become a battering ram at her temples.

"I don't know; maybe just talking about it makes it seem less . . . less—"

"Gross?"

Laughing more, "Yeah, less gross."

"Well, I'll tell you what, I have a really fabulous membership at the Y's new facility in Rancho Mirage, but I've been too busy to actually get my tush over there to use it. I'd be happy if you'd take it off my hands—if you'd promise to shoot over there and climb the rock wall for an hour after work every day and six times on Sunday." Beth had no reason to know that the osteoarthritis condition that had been developing all this winter and spring was making any kind of movement, let alone workout routines, difficult to bear. "What do you say? I mean, it's all paid up through next Christmas! You can't let it go to waste, but you *could* let it go to waist." Bonnie's eyes twinkled at the silliness.

Shaking her head, "Eee gads. . . . But you're actually serious?"

"Of course. I'm always serious." The outrageous face she made, including crossed eyes, underscored the indisputable. "So it's all settled?"

"Yes—I'll do it! Thank you so very much; you're a blessing to me, Bonnie, in every way

42

imaginable."

She could only smile. "You had some junk for me to sign?"

"Oh—yes, those memos you dictated earlier."

And so it went—the months and then more months, moving into several years.

The monthly meeting of the Desert Cancer Foundation ran a bit late on this particular evening; but now that Bonnie was home and could stretch out and relax, she did exactly the opposite by going straight to her office with a stack of papers. These were items containing all the members' suggestions for her to organize their annual Cancer Walk-a-thon along with addresses, phone numbers, email contacts, and everything else useable for seeing that everybody in the county knew about the event in time to participate. The money raised would benefit cancer patients who couldn't afford their chemotherapy treatments, so it ranked very high on Bonnie's list of important causes to support.

"This needs to appeal to kids as well as adults, so I'd better plan some kind of catchy logo for the T-shirts that will appeal to youngish persons as well as oldish ones. Let's see . . . Desert Cancer Foundation Walk-a-thon . . . a camel for the desert would be appropriate, maybe stick some jogging shoes on him? Some red or blue ones? Cool. If I can find some clip art on the computer, I could design the thing right now." Bonnie spent a while fiddling with files from her library of CDs until she came up with a cute ar-

rangement.

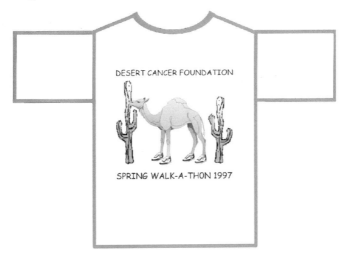

"Okay. I'll get this to the T-shirt print place tomorrow. And I can use the same image for all the hundreds of fliers I'll need for bulletin boards in supermarkets, libraries and churches, at Maric College, the high schools, health clubs and golf courses, and whatever else I can think of. Now let me think what else I have to do." She strolled to the kitchen for a cup of tea and then returned with ideas beginning to simmer. She needed to contact the area's radio and TV stations as well as The Desert Sun (the local newspaper), and various community men's and women's groups. "I have to get the word out as far as it can go because cancer patients who can't pay need the same kind of hope for healing that I have now—after a year since I was cured. People just can't live without hope."

"Is everyone here?" Bonnie asked above the

44

voices in her office. "So are we ready to finalize these preparations? Does everyone have coffee and multiple cookies?" She moved closer to the food table. "Kristen? Here's a cup for you, nice and hot. . . . Heidi? Did you get a turn up here with the goodies?" Several of Bonnie's staff members wound their way forward as others were settling into folding chairs in an loose circle around the room. "And here comes Beth with another box of donuts! . . . Ellen, you *need* one of these glazed ones! Come on, people—this is pig out time, required. Doris? Terry? How about you, Courtney? And is KaNeesha here?"

The hubbub lasted not long; after a few more minutes each had loaded a plate and found a seat, though the level of talk was hardly less intense.

"So! Shall we talk about the drug company's big Cancer Survivor Party while we munch?—that is, since the discussion's why we're hanging out munching in the first place? Maybe if we have reports from each of you about the area you've been covering, everybody will be up to speed. What do you have, Beth?"

Bonnie's assistant set her coffee cup on the floor. "The gigantic parking lot is reserved for all day Saturday, and the tent people will set up their tents first thing that morning. I've also taken care of those jillions of tables to be placed for the banquet and enough chairs for 900 people unfolded and ready to go." Pausing with a little laugh, "This is really a big deal, isn't it?"

"You can say that again. Aren't we glad we're not personally paying for it! Thanks, Beth, for such a masterful job on so many nasty de-

45

tails." Bonnie made a check mark on the list she had on a clip board.

Just then, before they could get any further, a buoyant head bobbed into the room. "Dr. Natarajan!" they exclaimed together and then laughed.

"Ladies, ladies, do not let me interrupt your meeting!"

"It's no interruption, Dr. N," Bonnie said at once. "We're just going over the final details of the drug company's big party on Saturday."

"Ah! I have no doubt that in all your capable hands the affair will be splendid—spectacular even! Will we have a good showing?"

"It certainly sounds like it."

"Well, I'll look forward to enjoying all the festivities. And what a positive statement we'll be making to the world, no?" He buzzed here and there and patted a few backs before spritzing out into the hall.

Bonnie smiled. "Looks like we're officially judged about-to-be successful. But meanwhile, what about you, Ellen? Did Dr. Lee take care of the flowers?"

"Yes, she did—big time. She has a sister in Hawaii who's going to send all the bouquets; and from what I gather, the arrangements will be pretty spectacular—birds of paradise, all that sort of exotic thing. And I think she's planning on having corsages for all the staff—us! yea!—and, even more, for those cancer survivors giving testimonies about their experiences and cures."

Bonnie couldn't help but add, "Yeah, anyone brave enough to stand up in front of that

46

many people and get personal about their cells and organs and meds *deserves* to be wearing flowers! . . . Thanks for arranging all that with Dr. Lee; you always know just how to motivate people." She made another check mark on her list. "Let's see, what *about* those people—Terry?"

She finished swallowing a bite of chocolate chip cookie. "I've had RSVPs from almost exactly 900 people, believe it or not (that is, they actually responded before the last minute). They're coming from all over California as well as Nevada and Arizona. And 23 of those have confirmed their intention of giving a little talk. I have the most up-to-date lists anyone's ever imagined. Don't you love it when folks take care of what they're supposed to?"

"Eee haw! . . . I wonder if maybe people who survive cancer develop a new perspective on life," Bonnie said quite casually, "—that is, maybe they take care of things without putting them off because they've learned about the brevity of time."

"Oooo, Bonnie!" Beth teased. "You talk like you know what you're talking about!" The odd truth was that no one in the room realized Bonnie had intimate familiarity with the subject at all. "But I guess every one of us should be aware of *time* like that even *without* having to get sick."

"Amen to that." Once Bonnie had made another check mark, she added, "Thank you so much, Terry, for keeping track of all those records. No kidding—dealing with that many people can be daunting, but you're always so good with thousands upon thousands of details."

She paused to look around the room. "Now, what about the food? KaNeesha and Heidi, you shared that horrendous job between you. How about it? Did the caterers come through?"

Heidi jumped right in. "Oh yeah, and how! We got Antoine Toubia's outfit in Palm Springs to work their magic; we're assured of having a feast fit for royalty."

"Yes, and I've lined up a number of homeless organizations to receive all the left over caviar and cream puffs," KaNeesha added with a laugh.

"That is just so cool. You two think of everything." Bonnie scanned her clip board and then cast her gaze around the room. "Courtney, are we scheduled with a cleanup crew, or should each of us bring a couple dozen big black trash bags and plan on staying really, *really* late?"

Smiling, "We're scheduled!—guaranteed! Don't any of you plan on pulling on all-nighter in the parking lot."

"Whew, we appreciate your taking care of that detail more than any other part of this shindig, believe me. Does anybody else agree?"

"Bravo!" and clapping met her words.

"Then, finally, Kristin? You shed your artistic talents over the invitations and took care of mailing them. Everyone has seen them, of course, but I wanted to acknowledge how nicely they turned out and thank you for accomplishing such a huge job."

"Yes," Terry piped, "I wouldn't have had those 900 on-time RSVPs if you hadn't gotten the notices out so early. They were very classy looking."

48

"Well, thank you both. I had a blast doing them." Kristin quickly looked down and took another sip of her latte.

"Ok guys, it sounds like we're pretty much ready to rock and roll. Will everybody be able to show up Saturday to wear those flowers, support the guests, and help the food disappear?"

Naturally each of them exclaimed agreement, for it was truly one of the biggest events of the year.

"Well then, our meeting's adjourned, so to speak. Nobody leaves until all the goodies are gone! . . . Any questions, comments, headaches, or hugs?"

There were, and they did.

"Happy Birthday, Mom," Bonnie exclaimed with a flourish of her arm. "And welcome to Egypt!— so to speak."

Before them rose a mighty sphinx, duplicating the original in everything but ancient age and proximity to the Nile. And just beyond loomed a bronze pyramid so vast and imposing that it dwarfed everything in the splendorous city around it. Indeed, the light spraying from the topmost point was the most powerful and brightest on earth and could be seen from not only several hundred miles away but possibly from earth orbit as well.

In other words, the Hotel Luxor in Las Vegas beckoned with a tantalizing vigor and promise of birthday celebrating just short of over-the-top. Never mind that the actual Egyptian Sphinx and Great Pyramid, both located on the Giza Plateau just outside of Cairo, were

49

hundreds of miles north of the real city of Luxor. The wonder of cramming everything Egyptian into one single spot on The Strip, call it poetic license if you will, seemed enough to take huge liberties with geography when so much fun could be the result. And this effect was certainly Bonnie's intention, as ever, to honor her mother, her best friend's special day.

"I have so much in mind, Mom; plan on being totally swept away."

"I always am; you just spoil me. But of course I wouldn't have it any other way."

At last they entered the pyramid and paused in wonder just inside. The vastness of buff colored marble and sheening gold made the height and breadth of it, the length and width and full effect something that all but caught their breath.

"Awesome," Bonnie murmured.

"It really is, isn't it?" her mother echoed.

"Let's hurry and check in over here so we can get on with our celebration. What d'you say?"

"Sounds perfect to me."

In a while they had taken care of that particular business, found their room (one overlooking the world's largest and most wondrous atrium and glowing with soothing gold and amber tones), and settled their luggage. Now they were ready for everything this newly created ancient city had to offer.

"So what shall we do first—the spa, the slots, the shops, a tour of King Tut's tomb and the works, or a meal?"

Smiling with complete happiness—for her

50

daughter was *well* and happy after three years since her treatments; these surroundings were opulent in the extreme; and the fact of being honored with such elegance seemed truly luxurious—Murra could only shake her head with a laugh. "How about all at once?"

"You're on!"

Before long they had reached the casino floor, a glittering festival of blinking light and motion, an area touted by the hotel as being "wide as the Nile," a place of treasure to be found as rich as any pharaoh's tomb had held. With a hand on her mother's arm, Bonnie paused just inside.

"Here's a part of your birthday gift, Mom," she said, handing her a gilt bag with a metallic drawstring closure. Smiling slyly, "Don't lose it all at one time!"

"What in the world?" She paused to open it. "A bag of nickels for the slot machines! Oh my, you know me too well."

"There's $20.00 in there. Just be sure you spread it around the room, okay?"

Laughing, "I'll be overjoyed to do just as you say. But aren't you going to help me lose it?"

"Not just now. I have an errand to do first; then I'll join you."

"All right. I'll get started pumping my arm, and you'll meet me back here, right?"

"Right. Absolutely."

"What's the errand, anyway?"

"A secret, O Nosey One."

Murra smiled at the delicious mystery and headed off toward the slots, hoping to try her luck at one with an Egyptian theme.

With no delay, Bonnie headed for the shopping mecca in the hotel, the Giza Galleria, a promenade fashioned like an Egyptian *souq* or bazaar. *"Mom likes jewelry; maybe I can find something truly special, maybe some earrings with a middle eastern flavor. I wonder what store would have such an item."*

She heard the plash of one fountain after another and marveled at the massive Egyptian statuary and frenzy of color awash across the way. Vendors and artisans competed for her attention with their wares. Here was one selling exotic perfume bottles and alabaster pottery; there another was stocked with papyrus papers decorated with hieroglyphs in gold (suitable for framing), and still another offered silver bangles and bracelets. She decided to look more closely at this last, to browse a bit and possibly chance upon some brilliant bit of perfection.

Finally she spotted a display with handcrafted earrings, just what she was hoping to find. *"Glorious!"* she reflected, examining one set in particular. *"The purest jade with intricate filigree curlicues in sterling silver. This is exquisite. Mom will have a fit."* At once Bonnie paid for the jewels and accepted them in a small velvet pouch of navy blue embellished with golden threads.

"Thank you so much for your beautiful work," she said to the artist handing her the treasure.

"You are most welcome, madam. I am originally from Jordan and used to sell my handicrafts in my family's shop in Amman. I feel hon-

52

ored you have chosen my work. Is it for yourself or for a gift?"

Smiling, "It's a birthday present for my mother—who just happens to be my best friend. Only the best is good enough for her."

The man bowed low, even from the waist. "Truly, you honor me."

"Thank you. I'll never forget you."

Suddenly minding his manners, "Ah, but you must have some of the best for yourself as well, madam! A pair of earrings of your own perhaps?"

"Well, I do love earrings above almost anything there is, but I want to keep this day for my mother alone. Next time!"

"*Salaam alaykum,*" he said, "Peace be unto you." The man touched his forehead with a flowing gesture outward.

"Thank you; that is, peace be unto you, too."

Bonnie slipped the little bag into a zippered compartment of her purse and set out to locate the rest of her purchases. *"Now I need something for all my girls at work; can't take a trip without bringing something back for my special friends."*

Casually she strolled along the stone walkways of this busy marketplace. Here she paused in the entrance of a shop called the Treasure Chamber. Inside lay artifacts and antiquities that appeared to have come from the tombs of kings and queens of ancient Egyptian dynasties flourishing some 5,000 years in the past. Were they actual riches dug up in the Valley of the Kings across the Nile from Luxor, or were they reproductions?

"Hmmm . . . a six bazillion dollar artifact for each of my girls? . . . Maybe not today." Smiling to herself, she continued her walk among the shops. *"Oooo—here's something cool."*

This store tantalized by scenting the air outward. What was it?—Candles? Incense? Soap? Bonnie followed her nose into the shop known as LeliaSea, one of the most unique skin care boutiques she had ever imagined. Pausing before an explanatory poster, she found that the products here came from the mineral rich area around the Dead Sea, the lowest body of water on the planet, situated between Israel on the west and Jordan on the east. Visitors to the spot could be seen covering themselves with mud along the shore because the unusual blending of minerals and salt found there was famous for its healing characteristics. And the marvelous products of LeliaSea were made from such materials. Bonnie was sure any one of them would make a well-received gift for her friends. But how to decide among them?

"Facial Mud Mask?" she wondered to herself. *"Black Mud? I wonder what someone would think about getting a jar of mud. . . . Ah, what about these nice little baskets of LeliaSea Bath Salt with Black Mud Soap? Fancy. And the tag does explain about why the mud is a biggy. Yes, these will be perfect."* Bonnie picked out nine of the elegant packages (an extra one for her mother in addition to those for her staff) and made several trips to the counter with her treasures to pay for them.

At last she was once more among the shop-

54

pers of the bazaar. *"I'd better get back to see how Mom is doing with her nickels. Hope she wins big for her birthday today!"* And before long she had walked across to the casino to begin her search.

Wandering among the multitude of slots, finally Bonnie saw a bit of a spectacle—and at the center of it her mother. Of all the odd events, here was Murra exclaiming and laughing as hundreds upon hundreds of nickels were foaming out of her current machine. She was trying to scoop them into a bucket; but because that little item was proving inadequate, the people around her were helping collect the coins in their own and presenting her the spoils with flourishes and more laughter.

"What on earth have you gone and done!" Bonnie whooped, joining in the hubbub. "I was just considering how totally cool it would be if you were to win something, but I figured it was just wishful thinking. But here you've up and broke' da bank."

Calming herself with a hand over her heart, "Why, Bonnie, isn't it just amazing? How much do you suppose is here, anyway?"

"Oodles and tons. It's great that everybody helped you (and didn't help themselves!), so let's go over to the desk area and see if we can get this changed into some paper bills."

In a few minutes they found the original $20 had paid out to $100, and the two of them could not stop laughing.

"So are you hungry, Mom?"

"Absolutely."

"Well, then how about the Pharaoh's

55

Pheast Buffet? They have just about everything a pharaoh or pharaoh-ess could think of. I hear they even have a 30-foot salad bar and gooey desserts."

"Mercy."

"My thoughts exactly."

Once they had reached the restaurant, chosen a table, and spent half the afternoon (or more) deciding what *not* to choose from the buffet, at last they settled themselves in grand style for a memorable lunch.

"Are you going to tell me what your secret errand was and if it has anything to do with all your interesting packages?" Murra began.

With a straight face, "No. Shall we get some more of this dreamy crab stuff?"

"Bon-nie!" she laughed. "You are too cruel."

"Okay then, Moth-er! You've got it." She rustled in her purse and one of the shopping bags. "Nothing's actually wrapped per se, but I'm sure you understand."

"Of course."

"Or—quick—I can wrap them in one of these spare napkins!" She scooped up one of the cloth beauties from the place setting at their table no one had used and wound it around one of the baskets of beauty products. "For you, Most Belovéd Mother—salts and mud!"

Murra scrutinized the items with a smile. "Mud, you say?" The explanation written in the tag held her interest for several minutes. "My, these sound lovely, Bonnie."

"Well, I got one of those for each of the girls at work and one for you; it's not your ac-

56

tual *birthday gift.*"

Laughing, "I see. Well, it's quite lovely anyway, dear."

"Here's the actual outcome of the errand." The small velvet pouch made its way from the purse compartment with a sort of serene grandeur. "It was crafted by the actual guy I got it from—a Jordanian artisan. He even spoke to me a little in Arabic."

Murra gasped at the exquisite earrings. "Oh my goodness, Bonnie. I can't believe how beautiful these are. And you say the fellow made them himself?"

"Yes, that's what he said. Can you imagine anyone having fantastic enough finger dexterity to pull off such creations?"

"It does seem almost too good to be true." Murra took a sip of her tea, a small hesitation as she continued to admire the jewelry. "You know, speaking of dexterity, we never actually talk about your condition—"

Frowning ever so slightly, "I don't have a condition."

"Well, that is, I mean the one you had three years ago. Dr. Natarajan has certainly proven he has that kind of ability with his hands to have made you so well. I mean, I'm sorry to bring it up, as ever, because I know you don't like to discuss it; but I want you to know how grateful I am to that man—and of course even more to the Lord God—that you're cured and healthy and back to being your old lively self."

Bonnie couldn't help but smile. "It's true I do feel wonderful."

"It does concern me that he doesn't do

more checkups; but every time I see him, he pats my back and says, 'Your daughter is doing so fine! And she does such exceptional work for my foundation! She is a prize, no?'"

Bonnie grinned with her whole face. "He said *that?* Too cool."

"Yes, and it's always so obvious how much you love working for him."

"To be honest, I don't actually see him that much. You know how busy he is with 75,000 things going on all at once, what with the cancer center and all his national and international doings; but there's no question how much I love the job. I really feel like I make a difference in people's lives, and who could ask for more?" She stretched a bit and then added, "So are we ready to hit the dessert buffet? We may as well do this right—you know, with the highest possible number of calories loaded in the most extravagant of cheat-items?"

"Lead on! We're really having ourselves a day, aren't we!"

Mid-morning, late fall. Bonnie's desk was piled high with well-sorted stacks of insurance forms and manila folders almost as if the entire contents of her filing cabinets had been chucked out of their snug alphabetical havens to be worked on all at once in this spot. Even more than cluttering, the paper seemed intent on combining forces to shove the bouquet of yellow spider mums and cattails off the desk altogether.

"*What a mess. It's like tax season for an accountant around this place today.*" Her hand patted here and there for the coffee mug she

58

was using—one depicting a gigantic wave hitting Hawaii's North Shore and with the inscription, "Climb Every Mountain!!"—and found it empty. With a sigh, Bonnie rolled back her chair and struggled to her feet, marking how the arthritic pain and these brittle bones seemed like living fire to her awareness; Bonnie reminded herself to call Dr. Cliffton, her bone specialist and old friend, for a refill on her medication. Meanwhile, she edged toward the coffee pot and found it also empty. Starting a new edition of the brew, Bonnie snacked on a small box of chocolate raisins and wiped off every surface in sight while the appliance fizzed and bubbled.

When the coffee was finished at last, she removed the filter with its soggy grounds and poured a cup to accompany her through this next set of insurance claims. The small stack she now approached held those few she sensed would be most difficult in that the companies might be refusing to cover the patients' various medical needs. Her whole heart cringed at having to bear such devastating news to the people involved. But just how bad would these rejected claims *be* this afternoon?

She picked up the first one. *"Horace Metcalf—oh yes, I remember this one all right: the horrendous blood disease with that complicated surgery during the summer."* She swept her vision down the page. *"But wait—this can't be right! One hundred thousand dollars for his ordeal and they're actually turning him down?!— something that saved his life? These companies can be tricky, but I can't believe something like this!"*

59

Bonnie rose and paced to the wall of windows opening to the courtyard at the front. *"I know this man will never be able to pay such a huge amount on his own. Few people could. What's the point of having insurance if the jerks won't approve catastrophic illnesses? Are people supposed to pick and choose what diseases they get? This is crazy."* Her gaze slanted with the sweep of wind in the palms outside. *"I could never have afforded my surgery or all those chemo treatments—stuff that certainly saved MY life—if insurance hadn't paid. What would I have done? What will poor Mr. Metcalf do?"*

Bonnie returned to her desk for some Tylenol for her headache. *"I can't just call him and start yapping at him about what's going to be a disaster in his life. But what can I do instead to help him? I need some kind of big guns."*

Staring out the window but seeing nothing but the inner workings of her mind, she thought, *"Mary Bono! Congresswoman from this 45th district, took over after her husband Sonny Bono died! (Imagine Sonny Bono as an elected official! 'I've got you, babe!') But still—she's on the subcommittee dealing with health, Medicare, insurance, and all that sort of junk and is one heck of a go-getter. Maybe she can do something!"* She hurried back to her computer. *"This letter will have to go out today even if I have to stay here all evening writing it—to get it just as perfect as it can be. So much will depend on it."*

Bonnie had watched the sun streak the heavens pastel peach swirled with vivid scarlet long ago; but the letter outlining Mr. Metcalf's illness,

60

treatment, and recovery along with his insurance company's denial of his claim had achieved physical form at last. Guided by a single desk lamp and the light from her computer screen in the darkness of the building, Bonnie worked slowly, painstakingly, with a fussy attention to each single word and its effects on every other word and paragraph and phrase. On her way out to her car, she mailed the envelope.

"If this letter does the trick, what could possibly be more satisfying than such a job as this? I would feel as great a participation in Mr. Metcalf's wellbeing as the surgeon who fixed up his blood in the first place. I'll keep my fingers crossed—all ten of them."

And a week later she received word from Congresswoman Bono's office that the patient's medical bill problem, indeed, would be resolved. Bonnie celebrated by calling the man herself with the good news and by buying a single red rose for all eight of the girls who worked for her.

Chapter Six

2001

A hot Sunday afternoon, early June. Bonnie finally set aside her cleaning brushes and mops, spray bottles and vacuum attachments—the normal equipment of every weekend of her adult life—and poured herself a glass of lemonade. A spotless house was a high priority for her, and the place gleamed with a white-tile and glassy-surface sort of sparkle.

While normally preferring the circular sofa, this time she settled into the recliner beside the fireplace and put up her feet. *"Peace,"* she thought. *"This is peace all the way down."* Her sight wandered from the stuffed critters sitting on the hearth nearby across to the two cacti—whimsically like two thumbs sticking up as if to say "You've come a long way, baby! Right on!"—residing on a wicker trunk. *"I really feel like sharing this happiness I feel. To celebrate my living almost five and a half years beyond that terrible cancer scare—to actually have made it this long. But who? And what?"*

Bonnie rose and paced across to the curio hutch, a stylish scroll-work one in creamy wrought iron, to gaze at the framed photographs and memorabilia displayed there. *"No question that Mom will be part of this, but who else shall I include?"* Her glance fell on a picture of her two brothers, and immediately her mind jumped

62

a generation and exclaimed "Jillian!" The daughter of her brother Gene, who lived in Wichita, Kansas, seemed immediately like the most perfect choice. *"She's old enough to remember (in later years) whatever trip we decide to take; and if we were to go just before school starts, she'd be free. But where? Disneyland? Nah, Gene and Charlene have already taken Jillian and Taylor to Disneyworld. . . . I need to think of something else—a place that would knock the socks off all three of us."*

She walked back to the fireside, her vision stroking over the rough sandstone image of a horse hung just above, a southwest decoration that always reminded her of one scrawled on the wall of some aboriginal cave; and the impression jiggled a bit and finally hit. *"Hawaii! A primitive and untamed paradise! Well, except that we'd be on the super sophisticated beach in a biggy hotel rather than out in the jungle, of course. But what a fantastic idea! Nothing could be better. We'll do it!"* Smiling to herself, she crossed to the telephone at once. *"Guess I'd better ask both of them before I make the reservations!"*

"Aunt Bonnie! Aren't the leis beautiful?" Upon entering the hotel, Jillian had beamed her small round face into the image of any of the cherubim you'd chance to meet on the sun side of a cloud and had bounced up and down a few times. "What are they, baby orchids? Do we get to keep them?"

"Absolutely, positively. It's the Hawaiian way of saying 'Aloha.'"

63

"What's 'aloha'?"

"Well, it's hello and goodbye and everything nice in between."

"So when I go back to school, if I go around saying 'aloha' to all my friends, it would be a good thing?"

With both arms around her little niece, "A very *very* good thing." Turning slightly, "What do you think, Mom?"

"It would be just about the best I could ever imagine. I recommend it."

Before long, they had checked into the Outrigger Waikiki Hotel and were following a porter behind their assortment of bags to the fifteenth floor, the side facing directly into the clear aquamarine of the Pacific. Once inside, the three sprayed across and flung open the wide window doors to the balcony.

"Oh Bonnie!" Murra began, "We're right on the beach—I mean, the sand is *right outside* here. And look—it's actually Diamond Head framing the scene at the end of the curve of sand, as advertised. This is just amazing."

Bonnie smiled softly, for this was the place on earth she held closest to her heart. "And it's all for you, Mom." Adding gently with a hug to this oldest and best friend, "I'm so thankful we could come here together, thankful that I was able to be cured, to go on living life."

Realizing how hard such a sentence was for her daughter, Murra hugged her back and murmured, "Me too, honey. Me too."

"Grandma, can we go swimming right away? The pool down there looks de-lic-ious."

"Why sweetheart, that sounds perfect to

64

me. We big girls can rest and be lazy after that long flight, and you can splash and holler after sitting still so well for so many hours. What do you think, Bonnie?"

"I totally agree. I'll even bet they serve margaritas down there by the pool! Shall we get ready and go see?"

"Goodie!" Jillian twisted her six year old self into a small tornado of motion as she dug through her suitcase and extracted her swimsuit with a flourish.

In a short while the three had gathered at poolside and were breathing in the clear sunny air. The water shimmered like blue jello; Jillian was already submerged in it and hooting at the sky. The palms surrounding the area swayed in the breeze, attuned to the beat of hearts; and with no delay the adults had stretched out in chaise lounges under them. Sipping their drinks, a sense of calm fell over them.

"Two whole weeks to loaf and sightsee the visions of paradise," Bonnie murmured.

"Life doesn't get any better than this, does it?"

"Not so far as I can tell. Wish we could plant ourselves here like some tall old palm trees, Mom, and just hang forever. You know—like a couple of cocoanuts."

Smiling, "I'm ready if you are. Sounds like a fine way of life to me."

Splash sounds interrupted their day dreams. "Aunt Bonnie! Look at me! Grandma! Watch me swim!"

The two chuckled. "Looks like we're being paged," they said almost together.

65

"You're getting very good at that, sweetheart," Murra called. "Your mommy and daddy would be very proud to see you."

"Watch me dive!" The little one scurried out of the shallow end, hastened to the other, and jumped feet first and holding her nose with no attempt at style.

"Eee-haw!" Bonnie whooped. "That's the spirit."

Quite gradually as they talked and laughed, the sun inched toward its creation of long shadows from the trees; and the breeze picked up a bit against their warm skin. Eventually, Jillian transferred her interest from the refreshment of water to the antics of a small turtle nosing through the greenery of a nearby flower bed. Meanwhile, the two grownups finished their margaritas as well as the ice cubes floating in them and talked about what short discovery trip around the islands they should do first. The volcano? The Honolulu zoo? Diamond Head crater? Walking simply along the beach? Surfing lessons? The wonder was that the merest whim could be their guide. And so the first day passed with nothing tangible but magic.

It was so far into the night that all three were sleeping soundly upon one of the last rest periods of the trip. Exhausted from ten days' worth of sightseeing during the daylight hours, they were cradled softly, luxuriously, and thoroughly in one of the best Hawaiian hotels' deepest goose down. Nobody stirred, not even to turn over or adjust a pillow. The night's blackness had settled for a contented stay.

66

Abruptly voices in the next room woke everyone at once. The neighbors' television had been jerked on and then louder, and the frantic voices of news anchors sprayed every word almost clearly through the wall.

"What on earth?" Bonnie's mind gasped. She sat up suddenly in bed and automatically threw a hand over her heart. "Mom? Jillian?—are you both all right?"

"Yes! But what's going on?" Murra turned on the light, and they glimpsed at the clock: only 2:58 in the morning.

"Sounds like a news cast. What kind of bozos would play their TV so loud?"

"Maybe we'd better turn ours on and see what's happening. The voices sound pretty urgent."

Yawning with a smile, "Be my guest, Mom."

Teasing, Murra pretended to stick her tongue out at her daughter as she got up to locate the remote and clicked on the set to CNN.

"And we're coming to you live," Wolf Blitzer was explaining, "from the scene outside here in New York. If you're just tuning in, we'll inform you that some twelve minutes ago, at 8:46 Eastern Standard Time, an airliner crashed into the North Tower at the World Trade Center. Here is another repeat of that footage. . . . It is unknown at this time if this was an accident or if— Oh my God! Another plane is hitting the South Tower—a direct hit!"

Bonnie and Murra, both with hands covering their mouths in disbelief, were staring at the bald face of history, a stroke that would change the world forever after in that single hour's span, something so shocking that the spirit despaired of taking it all in. And the wonder of it: an event so cosmically huge seen live the very moment it was happening on good old normal CNN.

"Can this be for real?" Bonnie began.

"Do you think it was an accident? With *two* planes hitting like that, it sure doesn't seem like any stupid mistake in steering."

"No, I don't think so either. Would it be something internal like the Oklahoma City bombing six years ago? Some kind of radical domestic terrorism?"

"I guess we'll just have to wait until they sort it all out."

They grew silent as the unforgettable images streamed across the screen. An hour after the second strike, the South Tower collapsed, some twenty minutes later, the North Tower. Then news of the Pentagon bombing began being reported. Then the plane crash in Pennsylvania. And so the morning and afternoon went.

Nobody thought of surfing lessons. No visitors combed the beach. No shoppers seized upon the exotic stores along the streets of paradise. Outrigger canoe rides were canceled. Luau fire pits went unlit. Waikiki, as with every city and village nationwide, became a ghost town while the citizens of the whole world stayed nailed to their TV sets in anguish.

And it was five days before any airline flights could leave the island to carry these visitors home. Life after that—in personally differing degrees—would hardly seem normal to anyone; Bonnie was no exception.

Chapter Seven

2002

Her office was flooded with a sweetness of morning light, a late spring shimmer; and Bonnie had just finished making the first pot of coffee of the day. Now she was sitting behind her desk arranging the various stacks of Medicare and insurance company files that she would worry over today, but she looked up when one of her staff persons poked through the door.

"You wanted to see me, Bonnie?"

"Oh, Courtney! Cool! Yes, come in and have a seat—after you pour yourself a cup of coffee. It's that wonderful hazelnut you like."

"How kind of you to think of it."

"You seemed a little bit down yesterday afternoon; just thought you might need a treat."

Courtney settled in one of the chairs facing the desk. "As ever, you guessed right."

"Is it anything you feel like talking about?"

"It's pretty embarrassing."

"You know you can tell me anything and I won't be judgmental."

"Well, it has to do with Billie."

"The new girl who started sitting across from you?"

Heavily, "Yes. Somehow she's managed to get herself appointed as God's Assistant, and everything she says to me is beyond negatively critical into downright nasty. At least that's how it seems."

"You feel like she thinks you're a moron?—whereas you and I both know you're completely the opposite?"

"Exactly!"

"What does she say, for instance?"

"Oh, stuff like 'Nobody wears their hair like that anymore' or 'Don't you think wearing red makes you look washed out?' or 'Your voice sounds terribly shrill on the phone' or 'Aren't you afraid that having flowers on your desk will give other people allergies?' or . . . I could go on and on."

"It sounds a little like the seventh grade: maybe she feels insecure in her new job and wants you to feel as miserable as she does."

"Yeah, seventh grade: that sounds reasonable; but I'm getting sick of it, Bonnie. I've started dreading coming to work. I'm afraid I take things like that personally."

"Well, good grief—she's *directing* them personally!"

Courtney smiled, "No kidding. Can you banish her to the basement or something?"

"Afraid not—she doesn't work for me. But in the interest of your health and well being, and along the lines of 'Don't Sweat the Small Stuff so You Don't Get Headaches,' what I'd suggest is to be as nice to her as you can pull off; I mean, really go out of your way to be kind and actively friendly. I don't know, shoot—if she doesn't have allergies, maybe buy some flowers for *her* and ask her out to lunch. Just ooze sweetness. Introduce her around your area; be a lifeline in her strange new world."

70

"You mean—fake it?"

"No, because that would make you feel resentful and bitter. Just be sweet to her and see if she's doesn't soften little by little into a genuine friend. At the same time, you'll be keeping your stress level and blood pressure down."

"But I feel like jabbing back—you know, getting even with her for making me feel so rotten."

Smiling, "I know you do! But maybe give the opposite direction a try."

"I guess I don't have anything to lose; it couldn't get much worse. . . . Thanks, as ever, for listening, Bonnie. I'll see what I can do."

"Cool. I'll be curious to see how well it works."

"Was there anything else you wanted to talk with me about?"

"Ah—yes, as a matter of fact. This report you gave me yesterday afternoon? This first column here? I believe you've added the fourth column to it instead of the third column. See the odd total here at the bottom?"

"Oh good grief! How did I mess up like that? I've done a hundred of those."

Bonnie smiled, "No biggy; don't worry about it. You've had the weight of the world lounging around on your shoulders this week."

"I'll fix it right away. I'm really sorry."

"It was a minor 'oops'; don't fret."

"Are you sure that—"

Interrupting, just then another individual hustled into the office with an air of fervency. Dr. Natarajan didn't take time to sit down but seemed content to hover around near the door.

71

"Greetings, ladies!" he hooted.

"Dr. N.! You're back from New York—how was the trip?"

"Splendid, absolutely splendid. But I have another paper to present this afternoon in San Francisco; I just stopped by to tell you hello and, I guess, as it turns out, goodbye at the same time."

Bonnie rose and walked across to the door. "You're the busiest man on planet earth. Your schedule makes everybody's head spin."

"Indeed! And mine also. Even still, I should be in the office tomorrow afternoon. I'm expecting some new equipment, a big new machine, to be delivered any day now; and I'm hoping to be on the premises when it arrives."

"That's terrific. What have you ordered for the—"

"Listen, sorry—I've got to run. See you tomorrow!"

And without ceremony, Dr. Natarajan flew out into the hall. Bonnie and Courtney watched through the large windows as he appeared in front of the building and hastened through the flowering courtyard to the parking lot beyond.

"I don't know how he keeps up that kind of pace," Bonnie observed.

"Gads, neither do I. But he seems to thrive on it." Courtney herself stepped into the corridor. "Again, thanks for listening, my friend; I'll give your approach a try."

"Great. See you soon."

Bonnie was just finishing the cup of hazelnut coffee she had enjoyed with Courtney when she

72

heard a number of distinct sirens converging out at the street. *"Sounds like a whopper of an accident,"* she thought to herself. *"I hope they get the person or people to the hospital in time to make them okay."* Then she opened the first folder in the Medicare pile and started to dig in.

In not many minutes she heard anxious voices outside her office, the hush of whispers and exclamations of news up and down the hall. What could be going on? At once Bonnie ducked out her door to find out.

"Beth!—What's all the commotion?"

"God, Bonnie, I just heard that Dr. Natarajan was in some sort of crash out there— just turning out of the parking lot apparently. Somebody ran the red light and hit him broadside; evidently he had shot out in front of that person without making sure the lane was clear. At least that's what I've been told."

Stricken, "Is he hurt badly?"

"Nobody seems to know. The ambulance just got here, and I think—"

"Yes! I heard the sirens."

"Shall we go out to the street and find out?"

"No, I don't think so; we'd just be adding to the confusion. Let's wait a few minutes, and I'm sure we'll hear something."

And, in fact, shortly Dr. Lee, an oncologist from the second floor, came by with the news; she was reporting generally to everyone standing in the hall. "I'm afraid he was pronounced dead at the scene," she said in a low voice.

"This can't be right," Bonnie murmured

as she leaned her back against the wall beside her door. "Things like this happen to other people, not to . . . that is, he was standing right *here* only a few minutes ago. How can this be? What kind of cruel joke is life playing around here?"

But it was not to be the end of unreasonable news.

Chapter Eight

2002

It seemed like everyone in the building was stopping by to see the delivery of Dr. Natarajan's order. Although the first week of June had dragged by since his death, still the voices kept low and the antics and joking of the staff held back as a sort of breathing memorial to him while they visited this interesting room on the first floor. Most individuals thought of the new purchase as a tribute in his honor and wanted to feel its presence as an extension of the man who no longer directed this place while whizzing through the halls.

In the world of medical equipment, the new Computed Tomography (CT) scanner being installed here at the Cancer Foundation of the Desert was absolutely top of the line. The unit resembled a gigantic donut fitted with a table that could slide through the hole or move up and down so the patient lying there could be viewed from all directions as the source of the x-rays rotated around him. Without question, such a device in a cancer treatment facility must be as important as the walls holding up the building; for it could allow images of tumors in multiple planes as well as three dimensions and, as a result, offer excellent opportunities for correct diagnoses.

Bonnie was acting as an informal hostess

as people came and went in paying their respects to the man represented by the new machine. Most spontaneously brought along a mug of coffee or a can of soda almost as a type of religious libation, although few were actually aware of the little ritual they were helping to celebrate.

"It's pretty downright incredible, isn't it?" said Dr. Lee, just entering.

"Absolutely true," Bonnie agreed. "How I wish Dr. N. could've been here to christen it."

"Yes, and to think how much this foundation of his has *grown*. He would've been so very proud."

"Looks like we'll have to carry on and be proud for him—to keep his memory and work alive."

The small crowd in the room milled around the unit and peered at the video monitors on the consoles inside a clear glass partition at the side, admiring the gleam of glossy white surfaces and remarking how "splendid" (Dr. Natarajan's word) everything looked. Nobody felt inclined to leave.

At last the technician who had been installing the equipment most of the afternoon signaled that he was finished. Everyone applauded, and the chat heightened.

"Somebody needs to volunteer to be the first guinea pig!" a voice boomed from over near the scanner.

"Yes! We need to test it before subjecting any patients to its clutches!"

"Who's game?"

"Anybody feeling brave?"

Bonnie, swept up in the moment, laughed,

76

"Hey—I'll donate my bod for such a worthy cause."

"Are you sure?" Dr. Lee asked.

"Completely. Come on—it'll be fun."

"Well then, tomorrow morning? Be there or be square?"

"You've got it."

The CT scanner lab sparkled with newness on this brilliant June morning. Bonnie, by arrangement, had come early to have her "just for fun" scan completed before work. Holly, the technician, bustled around getting this guinea pig ready in a hospital gown and settled on the table.

"I won't be injecting any dye for contrast, Bonnie," she said, "because we're not actually looking for anything. I'll just take a general hit at your front and back around the level of, say, your chest region to see if the machine's working okay. Then you can be off to solve the financial problems of everyone who walks through our outer doors."

"Sounds perfect to me. Can I have copies for my refrigerator door?—since they'll be famous as the first shots taken by our new machine?"

"You bet." She fussed with the dials and adjusted the table into the proper position. "I can have copies made for everyone on your Christmas card list, too, if you'd like."

"Fabulous idea; thanks, kiddo."

At last Holly moved behind the protective panel and started the unit's scanning in a spiral with X-rays. She worked meticulously, just as if a real patient were present whose life depended on the findings. And then she said, "All done. Great job."

"Great job yourself!" Grasping the ties at the back of the scanty gown, Bonnie sat up. "So, Miss Wise Person, when will the results be done and the copies be made so I can start addressing envelopes?"

"Well, dahling, I'll get the images to Dr. Hollander right away so he can play radiologist; and I imagine the protocol will demand that he get in touch with you himself. It's all very proper, or at least it's going to be when we get our act together."

"Your act already seems together in my opinion. . . . So sometime later today?"

"Oh, yes, I'm sure he'll get with you today."

The noon hour had just started, and Bonnie wasted no time in calling her friend, Angelina, to fill her in on the morning's pretend medical experience. But the details had hardly assumed audible form when a head poked into the doorway of her office. Here was Dr. Ron Hollander from radiology, apparently with the silly results.

"Gotta go, Angelina; I'll call you back." Bonnie set down the phone and turned her attention to the man now entering the room. "Ron! Come in and have a seat. Would you like some coffee?" She started to rise, but he waved her back down. "So, does the machine do everything it was cracked up to do? Does it *work?* I can't wait to hear about it."

His tight expression, abruptly noticed now rather than at first, sent ice cubes of adrenaline through Bonnie's veins. "Ron? What is it?"

78

"There's no easy way to say this."

"Say *what?* Something's wrong with the machine? No—something's wrong with *me;* is that what you're hedging about?"

"I'm afraid so. You know how we weren't looking for anything special and how Holly just aimed at a part of you at random—well, I'm afraid those random spots turned out to be areas of concern."

Her face blanched to the color of bone. "The cancer's returned?"

"Yes, it's metastasized; that is it—"

"It's spread."

He nodded and looked down.

"Where? How much?"

Dr. Hollander pulled the X-ray images from a large envelope. Pointing to one of them, he explained, "I found a mass—about a half inch in diameter—in the left lower lobe of your lung along with a nodule in the upper portion."

"Hey, that's not fair! I've never smoked a cigarette, a cigar, or a fumy old pipe; and this is the thanks I get?"

No smile cracked his face. "There's more." Bonnie's color faded even further. "There's a blastic lesion in the thoracic spine—that's the upper part of your back just below the neck." Hardly daring to look at her, "I'm so very sorry, Bonnie."

Shrugging ever so slightly, "So what happens now?"

"Since Dr. Natarajan won't be— that is, Dr. Menier will be taking over your case. I've given him copies of these findings and told him I would suggest your seeing him as soon as possible."

"Yes, I'll make an appointment now. Maybe I can even get in this afternoon."

"Good. I wouldn't wait. He'll want to do many more tests and get you started on some treatment."

"Truly cool! And thanks a bushel, Ron, for getting back with me so quickly."

Shaken by her pert reply, the man rose and dragged out of the office; for, as the bearer of bad news, he carried a weighty burden.

"Bonnie, I can't begin to tell you how sorry I am to be having this conversation," Dr. Menier began as soon as she entered his office later that day.

"Yeah, no kidding. What I can't understand is why Dr. N. didn't find any of this stuff sooner—I mean, before the crud had spread all thither and yon."

"Was he monitoring your condition right along?"

"Well—I *thought* he was. I know his busy schedule called him away a lot of the time, but—"

Softly, "Maybe we'd better not go there."

Bonnie looked down at the hands in her lap. "Maybe you're right. So where do we go from here?"

"I'm ordering a great number of tests so we can be sure of what we're dealing with, all to be done tomorrow or as soon after that as possible. We need to see what we can do to solve these and whatever other problems we may find."

Three days later Bonnie had returned to her new

80

doctor's office upstairs to learn the results of the various tests she had undergone.

"The pictures are all back, right? You have the results?" she said as soon as she was sitting down.

Dr. Menier's face looked grave. "Yes, and here's what we've found. The workup using the PET scan demonstrated a high-grade metabolic foci (that is, an area of increased metabolic activity—growth, in other words) in the left lung, the middle part of the chest, the space above the collarbone as well as the thoracic spine. The biopsy of the left lower lung demonstrated a lesion which indicates metastatic carcinoma. And the MRI of the thoracic spine showed a lesion at the level of T6 (around the level of the shoulder blades)."

"This can't be right! It can't possibly be!"

He shook his head. "And Bonnie, as you know, we did a further MRI on your head—because of your history of headaches and dizziness—and we found, I'm absolutely sickened to say, a lesion in the left occipital lobe (the back part of the brain) with surrounding edema and mass effect."

"Now you're saying I have a *brain tumor?* And with all this other junk—and I feel *terrific?* How on earth can this be?"

Softly, "The breast cancer from a few years ago has spread."

"Yeah, apparently," she quipped in a dry tone.

"But wait, Bonnie! We do have treatments. I'm going to start you on another round of chemotherapy, six or seven cycles, once every three weeks with the drugs Taxotere and Carboplatin."

"And that will do it, pouff, just like that?" She snapped her fingers.

"Not quite. I'll also refer you for gamma knife radiosurgery directed at that brain lesion and consultation for an opinion on its further management. You can take care of that in Los Angeles."

"What in the world is a gamma knife? That sounds about as non-thrilling as anything I can imagine."

"Great question: it's a helmet with holes punched in it, and the radiation is focused directly on the specific problem area and nowhere else."

"Charming. So I get to play space alien with an outfit like that?"

Chuckling, "Right on."

"Then take me to yer leader," she said with one hand raised in mock greeting."

Dr. Menier smiled faintly. "Yes, and I'd have to say that He's only one prayer away."

Chapter Nine

2002

Balloons, dozens of salmon and turquoise ones, hovered along the ceiling of Bonnie's office with long curly ribbons hanging down. Elivs Presley posters and memorabilia decked the walls as decorations in honor of her favorite icon, and absolutely everybody in the building either had already dropped by or was currently filling the room with high jinx and festivity not seen since the millennium bash celebrated by the whole world two years earlier. When Bonnie's friends and co-workers as well as her mother finally discovered how serious her condition was, they immediately threw her the biggest party they could imagine, a small gesture to express how very much she meant to them. Each in his or her own way was managing the utmost cheer, a complete fake; for it was only demonstrating how ripped up they felt inside and how greatly they needed not to let it show.

Dr. Hollander, the radiologist, had just finished an over-the-top Elvis impersonation that left everyone gasping for air, especially Bonnie.

"Elvis *lives!* He really *lives!*" she exclaimed, rubbing her sore eyes. "Ron, we didn't know about your secret identity."

"Yeah, Hollander, why would you hole up in a dank old lab when you could be giving the world back its King?" someone else insisted.

A number of the women formed a line by holding one another around the waist and jigged a bit to the tune and lyrics of "You can do anything, but lay off of my blue suede shooooes!" Laughing, "Hey, we could go on tour with Ron and be a band."

"We aren't playing any instruments."

"Well, our vocal backup is perfect without them! The Elvisettes."

"'Wise men say: only fools rush in.'"

"Who are you calling a fool?! Baby, we're on the way to the top!"

"More punch, anyone?"

"More peanut butter and banana sandwiches?" This came from Beth, Bonnie's assistant, who added, "Elvis's favorite, you know. Step right up!"

"Speech from Bonnie!"

"Speech! Speech!"

"You guys!—we're getting giddy here!" she laughed, trying to hold down the vital urge to vomit from the chemo. "You don't want a speech if it's going to be solemn; am I right?"

"It can be anything you want it to be. We just want to hear from you."

The room became more subdued, and eyes were directed to Bonnie.

"You have to know," she began, "how much this means to me—all of you, here like this. And even Elvis!" A small twitter of laughter pushed against the oppression they were feeling and jabbed a crack in the ice frozen around the subject of her illness. "I'm going to keep working even during the chemo treatments, barfing or no barfing. In other words, I'm going

84

to kick this thing—you just watch my smoke!"

"Hear, hear!" Everyone broke into the applause each really needed, a bit of closure on the tension in the room.

"Bonnie, we have a little something for you," Dr. Lee said, coming forward with two wrapped gifts. "Just a little expression of our love and concern."

Smiling, "You shouldn't have, but how totally cool that you did!"

Bonnie tore into the larger of the two and found a tremendous box of assorted See's chocolates—the premier variety on the west coast—along with a box of raisinettes. With a face full of deadpan humor, she spouted, "Ain't gonna have to share, am I?"

"Not on your life!"

"Oh Yes You Are!" Bonnie's mother came forward with a large hug in mind and with the most difficult cheer of her life manufactured on her face. The jolly tone of the party had weighed on her heavily, for Dr. Natarajan had always led her to believe Bonnie was in perfectly splendid health, and Bonnie herself had said nothing to alter that perception.

When the other package from the staff lost its wrappings, Bonnie discovered a little prayer book with soft pastel water color illustrations. She held it against her heart as she resumed, "And thank you for these sweet tokens. Looks like I'm going to get good and fat while talking with God! I'm sure He won't mind. And when you see me suddenly parading around here with a 75 inch waist, you'll know where it came from and won't mind a bit either!" She stopped in a fit of coughing.

"Well, Bonnie, some fats in your diet are supposed to be good for you," KaNeesha (one of her "girls") volunteered.

"Yeah, tootsie, omega-3 fatty acids found in fish oil, not chocolate cream filled bonbons!"

"Just tryin' to help."

Everyone laughed, and Bonnie started the three pound box of candy around the room. While the group became engaged with pretending to fight over the chocolates, Murra's gaze sought her daughter's; and when their eyes met and Bonnie's scared look registered, she could only think to herself, *"A valiant effort, sweet Bonnie, but I know this is all a fake. Nothing to be done about it, though; maybe faking is for the best. We're all doing the best we can with such tragedy as this."* Murra hid her concern in this current glass of punch. *"But what are her eyes saying? I have no doubt in the world that it's something like 'Why is this happening to me, Mom? Here I am: young, enjoying my job, living in the house of my dreams, happy as all get out, and feeling completely fit and well. This just isn't fair, and I can't believe it has anything to do with reality. What happened to Happily Ever After?'"*

In the midst of the chemo treatments and trips to Los Angeles for the gamma knife radiosurgery, one day Bonnie had to have a blood transfusion. She was feeling just as ill as during her similar nauseating therapy six years earlier, except that this time she was trying to work five hours each day as well. But this time after the

86

transfusion, her weakness seemed even worse. *"I'm not going to let this stupid situation keep me from living my life,"* she told herself as she unlocked the car and got ready to drive home. *"I'm going to lick this thing just like before."* She pulled out into traffic, the same spot at the edge of the parking lot where Dr. Natarajan had been killed. *"Just because the cancer's spread all over the place in my body doesn't mean I can't conquer it again; no way."* The cars foamed around her, but Bonnie kept her wits and held onto the wheel in the same cautious driving manner she had always maintained. And at last she reached home.

"How did it go? How are you?" Murra asked in meeting her at the front door.

"Happy as a clam at a dessert buffet, Mom."

"A dessert buffet?"

"Yeah, you know—nobody eats clams with cherries jubilee or pumpkin pie. *Happy,* get it?"

"Ah!" Her heart seemed to chill with doubt. "Do you want some dinner?"

"Maybe after a little while, thanks. First I need to get out of these clothes and, above all, have a hot bath in Epsom salts."

"Well, you just let me know when you're ready."

Bonnie headed for the bathroom to soak in the tub. *"Shall I tell Mom about the call I got today—that they've found two more brain lesions? . . . No. Why make it just that much harder on her having to watch me struggle?"* She slid down into the hot liquid with a shudder and a wave of nausea. *"Now I'm not going to upchuck in the bathtub, am I?"* She forced the sickening billow down.

Sometime later, she padded out to the living room in her shorty nightshirt and took her favorite spot on the curving sofa.

"All set?" her mother asked.

"You betcha; I feel fabulous. Hot water is the best invention since microwave popcorn. I think I could just *live* in it, a regular old crappie or tuna. Yes, and hallelujah, I'm as bald again as a sea bass." Bonnie placed her hand over her mouth, an unconscious attempt to keep the heaves from escaping.

"Are you ready for some supper?"

Lightly, "Oh, not quite. Why don't you come sit with me in here?"

"Would you like a nice backrub?"

"*That* would be pure heaven."

During these weeks of suffering, Murra spent much of the time working on her daughter's sore body. With Bonnie sitting on the floor in front of her, Murra's hands kneaded the back and marble-like head, the temples and jaw; for truly the cancer was everywhere and the aching was profound.

"So, Mother Dear, what little jaunt shall we take this weekend? Do you feel like going shopping in LA—say at Century City or Santa Monica? I'd love to look for some jazzy new turbans and maybe a new wig—a curly one this time; and I'm sure you need something pretty to wear for the rest of summer. If we don't hurry, the fall things will be in all the stores, and we'll be out of luck."

Murra knew better than to bring up her daughter's health and strength, but she jumped right in to humor her. "I wouldn't mind shopping in Palm Springs, Bonnie; we can find anything as wonderful there as in LA. I'd really rather try some place that's closer; I'm not sure I'm up for a long drive. Getting old, I guess."

"Old! Mom, you get younger every time I look at you!" She smiled but then quickly climbed to her feet and lunged for the bathroom, another bout of nausea working its way to the outside.

Murra watched her, shaking her head.

Before long Bonnie returned, and her mother continued the rubbing. "As we were saying, I suppose Palm Springs would be okay if you're really intent on no more than a fifteen minute drive. I really did want to get the ultimate wig, though."

"Well, my goodness, Palm Springs is one of the most elegant destinations around. People come make special trips *out here* to find the ultimate."

"You're right, of course. Guess I was just feeling adventuresome." Her rant of coughing lasted longer than her ability to breathe through it. "Sorry, Mom, I'm only—"

Just then the telephone rang as it did so often in the evening to bring the voices of Bonnie's devoted friends. "I'll get that in my room and be back in a flash."

She limped away stiffly and sank onto the bed with a sigh of pain. "Hello? Angelina! How sweet of you to call me!"

"You've been on my mind so much today even more than ever. How did the transfusion go?"

"Fabulously. High drama and theatrics."

89

"In other words, the usual crud?"

"That about does justice to it."

"I'm sorry for your having to endure all this, my friend. And did you hear the results of their newest hunt for additional brain tumors?"

"They found two more."

"That's just incredible. Will you be getting more extended gamma knife treatments now?"

"Yes, I'm set up to have one on Friday in LA."

"Good. Would you like some company on that long drive? I can take a day's vacation, no problem."

"Thank you for the kind thought, but I couldn't let you do that."

"Why the hell not!? I would do absolutely anything in this world to help you feel better, no qualification. You've been the best of friends to me; I just want you to get back to being yourself."

"Okay then, Ange, you're on. . . . I'm completely blessed to have such a friend as you."

"No, tootsie, *I'm* the one who's blessed. But listen, tell me how you feel about this news, I mean about the two additional tumors."

"I don't know what to do with it."

A pause. "Bonn, I hardly know what to say either."

"Well, your just *listening* means the world to me; you know you're the only one I can talk to about the worst parts of reality. I don't have a clue what I'd do without you. And I don't mean that as any disrespect to my mother."

"Of course not. I understand perfectly why you can't tell her all the nastiest stuff—to protect her, knowing how deeply she loves and

90

worries about you."

"I can't hurt her with the truth. I only hope it doesn't hurt her more if she finds out someday how much worse my condition is becoming than I've been letting on."

"Yes, but Bonnie, don't you think it's mostly the chemo that's ripping you apart so much right now? You were feeling pretty glorious before you started getting the treatments. And I'd expect that you'll feel just that great when you stop having to take them. Am I right?"

"I think so; I have to *hope* so." A short knock sounded just outside. "Hold on a second, Angelina; let me see what Mom wants out there." Bonnie rose from the bed's haven and stuck her head out the door. "Hi Mom, what's up?"

"Oh I wasn't sure if you were still on the phone; I don't want to be interrupting you."

"Never fret. It's Angelina, and we were just about to call it a night. I'll just be a minute."

"Okay, Bonnie."

"Hey, Angelina, I'll call you back later in the evening. I think Mom has some supper ready for us, and I don't want to disappoint her,"

"I understand. Have a great feast, so to speak."

"Yes, I just hope I can manage to eat something."

And so the rest of the evening crept along.

The little fir tree sat expectantly to the right of the fire place, waiting for the lights and baubles that would fulfill its life's meaning. A fluffy Santa bear lounged near the tree's toes and kept clearing his throat in readiness for the yuletide carols he was hoping to sing. And dozens upon dozens of Christmas cards hung on ribbons nearby, proclaiming the season's cheer from friends who wished healthful thoughts in this difficult year.

Bonnie was stretched upon the curving sofa and wrapped snugly in an afghan crocheted by three of her friends at work (each had done several stripes in a different color so the pattern would have variety as well as express multiple examples of love). The firelight felt drowsy, and the ambrosial aromas from the kitchen were adding to the cozy effect; but she had been trying to keep herself from nodding off. Christmas, the best part of the year, needed to be *celebrated*, not slept through by some invalid.

"What smells so good, Mom?" she called.

Murra strolled into the living room with a plate of cookies. "Why I've just made your favorite gingerbread boys and Russian tea cakes. I hope you've worked up an appetite."

"What, by hanging out here on the couch?" She cast a hand over her mouth and considered whether or not she needed to burst toward the bathroom.

"Oh, even just the smell of fir makes my mouth water for peppermint and gooey things," Murra said.

"Well, you're certainly right about that." Her whole body ached as if the bones themselves were moaning. "Shall we jump around and trim the little tree in question?"

"A great idea. I got the decorations down from the closet this morning while you were at work, so they're all ready." Murra pulled sev-

92

eral cardboard boxes from under the dining room table.

Bonnie smiled deeply at seeing the old friends from her childhood. Here was the painted glass bird with its soft filament tail, and here were the two glittery little elves, Pixie and Dixie, that she had always pretended helped Santa poke the dents into lego blocks. She gathered all three and hung them prominently at the front of the tree.

"Let's 'deck the halls with boughs of holly, fa-la-la-la-la-la-la-la-la!'" she sang. "'Tis the season to be rowdy, fa-la—'"

"Rowdy?" Murra was trying to untangle a string of lights. "Rowdy, did you say?"

"Yeah! We could streak through the heavens with our boisterous carols, or hang the lights outside on the house in this very hour."

"Um, Bonnie. . . . "

"Maybe a short walk to the end of the street in a little while?"

Murra did not say "Are you sure you're up to it?" but settled on "I believe my old bones could handle that; sounds perfect. Would you like some of these cookies?"

"In a minute, thanks." Bonnie picked up the sweet fuzzy snowman ornament that had figured heavily in her youthful games beneath the tree. She could only sigh at its slightly mashed little face. And then her mood dropped all the way down.

"Bonnie? Are you okay?"

"Yeah. Yeah, I'm fine. 'Fa-la-la-la-la-la-la-la-la.'"

"No, really. You suddenly looked so sad."

93

"I can't talk about it. I don't think I—"

"Maybe this once, in the softest voice imaginable so hardly anyone will hear?"

"I don't know. . . ." She reached for the old stocking monkey who always sat on the hearth waiting for Santa. Bonnie fingered his button eyes, and then her own eyes filled with tears.

Murra watched her daughter in sorrow. Was she feeling that visiting all these old friends made her wonder if she would ever see any of them again, if this would be the last Christmas? Murra felt shocked at the pain of such thoughts. "Are you sure you don't want to talk about it?"

Bonnie paused, then straightened up from placing the monkey in his favorite spot. "No. And I feel fine, really. I'm going to kick this disease just like I did last time. I control it. It doesn't control me. Period."

Smiling, but not able to breathe, "I'm sure you will, Bonnie. You're a fighter, a warrior. Everybody who knows you says so because we understand your strength. It's going to be wonderful, I'm sure, as soon as these chemo treatments get out of the way."

"You can bank on it." She began helping her mother hang the lights, but in a moment a wave of weakness slid over her. "In the meantime, would you mind finishing decking the tree while I lie down over here and admire your work? I need to rest up a little for our walk."

"Certainly, I'd be delighted. Here, let me set these cookies closer so you can reach them."

"Thanks, Mom. You take such good care of me." A spurt of what tasted like bile shot up

Bonnie's throat and made her gag. And in the whole evening she never did manage to get one of those cookie confections down.

Before long the small tree was strutting its finery, and the room shimmered with its holiday garlands and wreaths. At last Murra sat down and reached for a cookie.

"Maybe we'd better call Gene and Charlene in Wichita, Bonnie. I think they've been half-way expecting us to drop in during the Christmas break."

"Oops. . . . Big oops. I don't think I've gotten around to telling them about my resumed chemo treatments. They won't understand why we're not jet-setting into Mid-Continent airport any minute now. I feel bad—do you think they'll be upset? I especially wouldn't want to disappoint little Jillian."

"Not if we explain a bit."

"I have some gifts ready to send, Mom. Will that be enough?"

"They're family, honey. I'm sure they'll understand."

"Then merry Christmas to us all."

"And happy new year, Bonnie."

"Yes, I hope so. I certainly do hope so."

"Say, Mom, are you all right?"

"Just a little stiff."

"Stiff! You can hardly move. Here, let me take those decorations down; you look like a sparrow trying to work a jack hammer."

"That bad!"

"What is it, do you think?"

"An arthritis flare-up, no question about

it. I could hardly get dressed this morning."

"You just sit and I'll finish here." Bonnie took over the garland and wreath removal from the walls. Since she had already thrown up recently, she hoped that would satisfy her quota for this lazy Sunday afternoon and leave her free to help her mother.

"Are you up to it?"

Coughing, "Never better. Um, that is . . . the best I've felt since six months ago when I started this cycle of treatments. But of course this is nothing compared with how mah-velous I'll be feeling in a few weeks when I'm finished with them."

"I've been counting the days."

"Yes, me too. But listen, Mom, I want to take you to a specialist for that arthritis; maybe I can get you an appointment for tomorrow if someone's able to squeeze you in at short notice. You've been taking care of me all this time, and I can't help but wonder if the extra work has weakened you—or at least your joints. Now it's my turn to look after *you.*"

"But Bonnie—"

"No 'buts,' tootsie. You have to let me take a turn." She set a few tree ornaments in a box and started to undo the lights, but then she decided to take a short rest break on the sofa. "I'm not tired; I'm *thinking,*" she quipped. "I'll get all that finished in a little while."

Monday afternoon. Bonnie took off work so she could drive her mother to the doctor and be available for support, and now she was sitting in the waiting room while Murra was being seen.

96

Did the fact that she had no hair or eyelashes keep her from participating in life where the public could see? No way. She had the snazziest of turbans—a cocoa brown and cream abstract design to blend with the tailored pantsuit she wore—and felt a fine satisfaction in being able to do this as a loving daughter for the mother she adored.

"This is the way it was supposed to be in the grand scheme of things in our lives—with me taking care of her and not the stupid other way around. Maybe I'll honestly feel terrific once I'm not swimming in meds. Life will be wonderful again; I just know it."

Just then she heard someone speak her name; and when she looked up from the current issue of *People Magazine,* a familiar face filled her view. "Why, Erin Smalley! What are you doing out this direction?"

The petite woman, a former cancer patient treated at the Cancer Foundation of the Desert where Bonnie had taken care of her insurance forms several years in the past, sat down on the chair beside Bonnie with a laugh. "Oh—I just finished joining my sister for lunch; she's working here. What about you?"

"My mother's arthritis is giving her fits. I thought Dr. Fishman might be able to help." Bonnie paused. "You're looking awfully perky, Erin; are you still in remission?"

"Yes, absolutely. It's been almost four years now since I was first diagnosed. It's amazing to feel part of things again. But Bonnie—I almost hesitate to ask—are you undergoing cancer treatments? I guess it's the turban. Well, I mean, it's very chic in its own right, but I wondered—"

"No, that's okay, you're right." Bonnie deliberately chose not to tell her that she was experiencing cancer metastasized from a much earlier tumor event; there was no point in causing her friend worry about her own case. "But it's very well controlled, and I'm convinced I'll be as cured as you are before long. I'm having my last treatment in the cycle in a couple of weeks; and after that I know there'll be reason to celebrate. In other words, Eeee-haw!"

"That's what I've always loved about you, Bonnie. You're always so inspirationally positive. That kind of outlook will help you heal, too—good vibes make a healthy body—or something like that. Take it from one who knows: it may seem overwhelming right now, but you're going to feel better soon—when you can start living again with hope."

Certainly it was awkward letting this friend believe she was new to the disease and could use any advice about coping that someone could give her, but Bonnie stuck to her original little plan: she would not introduce the subject of cancer's possible return into this conversation. "Yes, thank you, Erin. I'm looking forward to that." Smiling brightly, "It sure appears you're doing everything right to have such a bloom of health. Are you wolfing down great quantities of fresh items and blue/green algae, or what?"

"Yes, I'm on a pretty strict regimen, a diet that would keep away any disease you could name. How about you?"

98

Laughing, "I've been *advised,* but I'm afraid I'm doing more barfing than eating these days. *Soon,* though, I'll be the Tofu and Sprout Queen of the Desert—along with you, of course. You'd share your crown, right?"

"You bet."

At this moment Murra appeared from the hallway across and joined the two in the waiting room. "Oh, Mom! I'd like you to meet my friend, Erin Smalley. She's someone I know from work. And Erin, this is my mother, Murra Kenneford."

While the two exchanged greetings, Bonnie stood up. "I guess we'd better head back, Mom, and get you started on whatever medication the doctor's prescribed. I'm anxious to hear all about the appointment." Pausing to give her friend a hug, Bonnie added, "Sorry to leave you so suddenly, Erin."

"Oh, no problem. I understand."

"It was super seeing you and finding that you're doing so well and looking so beautiful."

"Thank you, Bonnie. I'll pray for you to be just this well too."

Chapter Ten

2003

The daffodils just settled on Bonnie's desk—a gift from the little group who worked for her—proclaimed the arrival of spring. She moved around the room humming and watering plants while sipping coffee now and then whenever she passed the side table. Dr. Menier had asked her to stop by his office today because she had finished the seventh in the series of chemo treatments three weeks ago, and he wanted to discuss his plans for their next step in the process of getting her well. *"I can't believe that I feel semi-not-awful today. Maybe it's because the chemo-crud is working itself out of my system and keeping me barf-free for whole hours at a time. And then there are these fantastic flowers!—the best and sweetest scent in creation."*

Just then one of her group breezed into the office. "Hey, Bonnie! I see you got the flowers," Kristin began.

"Hey yourself, my ridiculously artistic friend. Yes! Aren't they amazing? How goes it?"

"It goes great. You certainly look chipper."

"I *am*—in fact, I'm about as chipper as a slug in a chrysanthemum field."

Smiling, "That's a good thing, right?"

"You'd better believe it. But what can I do for you?"

"Oh, nothing really. I actually came down

100

here to thank you for all your wonderful encouragement on that last project I had—that heavy duty design for the brochure cover?"

"Yes, I remember how you were having one of your insecure fits about the gorgeous images you'd drawn and I was able to browbeat you into submitting to my point of view—that your design was over the top in being not only perfect for the job but true art as well."

Kristin laughed outright and reached over to give Bonnie a hug. "What would I ever do without your cheering me on? You make me feel like the most talented person alive."

"Well, you *are* the most talented person alive. In fact, I think you should have an art show with all your paintings on display. Picture this—" Bonnie swept her arm across an imaginary panorama before them, "my patio set up with easels, folks dressed to the teeth in lace and new shoes, flutes of champagne set out with stuffed mushrooms and chocolate strawberries, and wallets bulging with the big bucks everyone will want to pay for your extraordinary stuff. What d'you say?"

Laughing with all the joy of being lavishly appreciated, "Oh Bonnie! What a thought!"

"Well, the offer's on—at least it will be as soon as I'm through with my chemo treatments and don't have to spend most of my time sprinting to the bathroom and wiping off my chin."

With another hug, "You're just the best friend, the very best."

"I'm blessed knowing you too, sweet one."

"Listen, I'd better scoot and get some work done. Hope you have a terrific rest of the day."

"You too, Kristin. Take care."

"Well, Bonnie, I think you'll like what I'm going to say," Dr. Menier proclaimed when she walked into his office. He was leaning his tall frame against the front of his more than cluttered desk.

"With an announcement like that, I'm *sure* I will. So does this story have a happy ending?"

"I don't know about *endings*, but I've decided not to have you continue with the chemotherapy, at least for awhile. I'm here to urge you to take a big, extravagant trip, something to rest and find some peace for yourself again. To get back to being *you.*"

"Oh Brad, that's just fantastic! I can hardly believe what you're saying!"

If he had any misgivings about her condition, the good doctor kept them to himself and only shared in the delighted feelings Bonnie was sprinkling over the room. "Do you have anywhere wonderful in mind?"

Without a second's hesitation, "Hawaii! It can only be Hawaii."

"Well, be sure to send me a post card," he smiled.

"Post card nothing. I'll bring you back a whole outrigger canoe and four guys to paddle it for such great news as this is!"

Beaming, "And I'll display it (them) proudly over my mantel."

"You'd better start construction immediately for a larger one."

"The crew is due to show up right after work today."

Both paused and looked at one another,

102

then started laughing at the nonsense. The moment—as pure in its joy as any could possibly be—was just magic.

When Bonnie got out in the hall, she began dancing along—not at a quick pace, for the pain deep in her bones was ever-present—but with a zest that comes from being high on life. She sang in her mind as she traipsed to the elevator, *"No more treatments! That means I'm well! I'm really well! How can I contain what I feel? If I could bottle it and give it to the world, we'd have everlasting happiness for everybody, absolutely everybody."*

Bonnie, now that she was home, sat down with her mother and some maps of the islands for a cup of celebration tea.

"So you say it's time for another trip to Hawaii?" Murra asked her.

"Yes, and I can't think of anything that would be more welcome. An end to this nightmare of debilitation. I feel so free I could sail over the city without any need for wings."

"And I'm just that happy for you."

She began sorting through the maps and brochures. "I'd like to invite somebody to go with us."

"Oh, Bonnie, I don't need to go again this time. I'd just as soon stay here and take care of the house."

"Is it the arthritis?"

"Well, dear, if the truth be told. . . ."

"I'm so sorry, Mom. I hate it when you don't feel good. But how will you take care of things if it hurts you to move around? If you're determined to stay, you would just have to let the house go to pot."

"Not *your* house! You always keep it so immaculate."

"I wouldn't mind if it stayed a pigsty, Mom, if it meant you didn't have to lift a finger or toe. I could schedule a housekeeping person to come and spiffy things up just before I returned if that would make you feel any better. I'd still rather have you come along."

"Next time!" She reached for her teacup. "But who should be invited?"

Bonnie had a sip of her tea as well, pausing to think. Then, at a stroke, she said, "Michelle, Cindie, and LouAnn!"

"Your cousins from Canada—what a great idea. That sounds perfect to me. Just think of all the catching up you'll have to do!—how long has it been?"

"Years! Too long. But do you think they'd not want to be seen with a bald and eyelash-less lady?"

With a laugh, "They'd be glad to see you in any condition."

"Then I'll go give them a call, Mom; and then we can—" Just then the phone rang an interruption to her thought. "Oops. Guess I'll do the calling after I take *this* call."

"Bet it's Angelina."

Smiling, "Yes, I'll bet it is, too."

And it turned out that Bonnie spent most of the evening on the telephone with these particular four of the people she loved.

The flights from Calgary and Los Angeles had

landed in Honolulu within a few hours of each other. Bonnie had arrived first and later met her cousins in the lobby of the Hilton Hawaiian Village Resort. Once everyone had checked in, unpacked in the spacious suite of the Ali'i Tower, savored the wind-whispered balcony overlooking a seemingly infinite expanse of Pacific blue, and had changed clothes, the little group was ready to relax in the beauties of this tropical paradise.

Just beyond the welcome center lounged one of the small lagoons with a path separating it from one of the largest and most crystalline pools in Waikiki. As they strolled along in the twilight and paused here and there to admire the splendor, the chat was light as they all got used to one another's company after so long an absence.

"Bonnie, this is the most gorgeous place in the world!" Cindie exclaimed. "I know you've been to Hawaii a number of times, but have you stayed in this particular hotel before?"

She had been enjoying the Japanese koi mouthing bubbles into the water beside their feet. "No, I've always tried to stay at different places so my memories of different trips don't get mixed up. These fine golden fishies and that wonderful waterfall over there will always serve as a backdrop for your three faces."

"How cool is that!" said Michelle.

LouAnn laughed. "Yeah, and we're sure to appear extra glamorous in your thoughts with all this romantic low lighting. Nobody gets to remember any of us with our hair in rollers. Do we have a deal?"

The four slapped high-fives in the center. "Deal!"

"So, ladies, shall we get ourselves a pitcher of margaritas and let the good times roll?"

"That sounds as fantastic as anything I've ever heard." Michelle took Bonnie's arm, and the others lined up in the same way, four across.

Cindie unleashed a few polka steps and blurted, "Oh guys, remember how we used to hang on like this and dance all the way up from the barn?"

"And Grandfather used to laugh at us until his eyes watered?" Bonnie added.

Michelle smiled with her whole face. "Yes, but we're not going to enter the Rainbow Lanai I spotted over there like a bunch of wild kids. They'd never serve us drinks."

"And that's something this celebration can't do without, right Bonnie?"

"Absolutely right."

In a few minutes the group entered the restaurant, behaving like grownups—though not highfalutin ones—and made their way to a table overlooking the darkening beach. As they settled, their eyes reveled in views of Diamond Head framed in purple sunset hues as well as, closer, dark silhouettes of palm trees dotting the sand, a sail boat decorated with white lights lolling just out from shore, and the lights of the string of hotels along the strand glittering in the restless swash of the waves. The four sank luxuriously into their chairs and let this long day of travel and luggage roll off their bodies as the margaritas were served with shrimp appetizers on the side.

106

Bonnie adjusted her tropical flower print turban and smiled with a serene sense that life had never been so perfect as this. *"Hmmm, and with the tequila in these drinks, it's getting perfect-er by the minute!"* she quipped to herself. *"How lovely to see these cousins again and to be surrounded by such balmy air and feeling great health! Wish I had some hair!"*

"What are you thinking about so seriously, Bonnie-bon? You look pensive," Cindie said after a bit of a pause.

Smiling, "Just how totally and completely peaceful I feel right now and how cool it is for us all to be together again."

"I'll drink to that!" Everyone agreed and clinked their glasses for another toast. "To peace and us!"

"You know, it's weird how peace is so much easier when you're a kid," Cindie began. "Life doesn't seem to make the fairy tale 'happily ever after' happen very often, does it?"

"You can say that again." LouAnn fiddled with her fork a bit. "It hasn't turned out very well, at least not the way I expected."

"Yeah, if you scratch beneath the surface of even the most beautiful life, you find pain— the one true constant." Michelle's forehead pleated together with the thought.

"Ah, yes!" Bonne smiled, "but I think the point is to force beauty to cooperate by not giving in to the pain. I know it sounds like a cliché to mumble stuff about 'Rise Above It,' but the way I see it: we can either have pain and be miserable or have pain and be happy in spite of it."

"Yes, to choose our reaction to the nastiness life inevitably throws at us. I like that." Cindie raised her glass again to punctuate her statement.

"But some of us are better at doing that than others," LouAnn said softly.

"Gads, listen to us!" Michelle cried. "How can we be sitting smack in the middle of heaven-on-earth and dragging out such sentences of gloom and doom?"

A pause of silence took hold, not an awkward one but one pregnant with thought. Finally, Bonnie filled the expectancy they all were feeling. "Maybe we need to clear the air, sweet ones. We haven't been in touch for months and—"

"Years! At least all together in person."

"Right, exactly. . . . So you haven't really been aware of why I'm wearing this turban. The truth is, the cancer I had six years ago has—"

"Wait a minute!" the three exclaimed almost at once. "You never told us about having cancer, Bonnie! What's all that about?"

Bonnie glanced down at her hands. "Well, I hardly told *anybody;* nobody at work knew, really nobody *at all* knew except Mom, my friend Angelina, and my doctors. I was sure I could conquer it, and—as I was just saying—I believed I could go on and have a satisfying life even *with* the disease."

"So what you're saying is that you have that turban because the cancer has *returned?*" Cindie spoke for them all.

"Yes, but I'm finished with the treatments now, and the doctor told me to go off on some wild and extravagant trip to celebrate. I couldn't think of anyone I'd rather do that with than *you,*

108

and here we are—getting swacked at the gates of paradise."

"Hallelujah!"

"Yeah!"

"But Bonnie, how do you *feel*?" Michelle reached her hand over to lay it on Bonnie's arm.

"Fabulous! It's one of the grandest highs in life to be snatched back from the pit, so to speak. It makes every minute seem ringed with magic fire."

"What a beautiful way to put it." LouAnn smiled, then laughed at her next thought. "Speaking of that, girls, do you remember the time the barn down the road caught fire? How we were climbing the trees in the orchard and sliding to the ground on the branches as they bent low?"

"Yes! We could see the flames from high in the trees. . . . Seems like yesterday afternoon."

"I remember the tanning our ears got from the tree maneuvers just as vividly."

Bonnie caught up the thought. "And the similar ear-shellacking we got after tying you to the tree, Michelle? You weren't very happy, and pretty soon *we* were even more not happy. Couldn't hear straight for the rest of the week."

"But Grandfather was a lot of fun more often than he was hell bent on disciplining his four little renegade granddaughters. Remember the time he piled us in that little sleigh and pulled us behind the wagon?" Cindie shook her head with the tenderness of the memory.

"And all that ice cream he pumped into us on those great drives into town? Strawberry and chocolate chip!" Bonnie smiled. "Life didn't ever need to be any more perfect than that."

"Yes, and as you were saying, it really doesn't need to be any more perfect than *this*, right here and now." LouAnn voiced the sentiment, and everybody nodded with a serenity that was chosen and completely self-aware.

The meal, with its festoons of cocoanut and pineapple, followed in a similar fashion. And in fact, the rest of the week while the four were together moved to the rhythms of peace and soul-filled fellowship while basking in more balmy sun than any of them had ever enjoyed. But at last it was at an end.

"Thanks, Bonnie," said Cindie at the end of a hug. "This has been more of a delight than any of us can express."

"We love you, Bonnie dear. You take care of yourself and keep us up-to-date on the progress of your recovery." Michelle dabbed at the corners of her eyes.

"And have a safe flight over to Kauai and a fun time next week," LouAnn added. "Thanks for absolutely everything."

"It's been my perfect pleasure. Have a safe flight to Calgary, too, girls. I love you all."

And before long, those two very different flights in two directions soared into the sky and disappeared from one another's view.

Bonnie's plane was taxiing to a stop at the Lihue Airport on Kauai, the western most island in the Hawaiian chain, the one to the west of Oahu. Her face was pressed close to the glass as hope of seeing her old friend Renee on the waiting deck feathered her mind. *"Will I be able to spot*

110

her? Will Chuck and the kids be with her? How long has it been, anyway, since we've been together back home?"

At last the plane came to a stop on the tarmac, and the occupants of the cabin erupted into motion. Overhead compartments spilled out and their small doors banged with muffled thuds. Voices and laughter affirmed that these people were glad to be in this place at this most excellent time.

Before long, Bonnie had descended the boarding stairs and crossed to the terminal. Almost immediately she was being pummeled with hugs from Renee Chalmers, one of her oldest friends, and her daughter Lucy.

"Bonnie, you look terrific. I can see that you've had no sun on Waikiki whatsoever!"

Laughing as they made their way to the baggage carousal, "Yes, a miserable time was had by all. . . . Goodness, Lucy, I absolutely cannot believe how tall you've gotten—and so beautiful and fit. Your mother tells me that you surf at the beach three blocks away, poor creature. My niece, Jillian, is about your age; and I know she would drool all the way from Kansas to Kauai with envy to have such an opportunity in life as that."

An outgoing child, still Lucy blushed a bit and said, "It's pretty terrific all right. But Jillian can come visit any time she wants. I could teach her to surf or ride the smaller waves in on a boogie board! We'd have a blast."

"I'll keep that in mind, honey. I'm sure she'd love it."

Renee reached for the suitcase Bonnie indicated, and the three began walking toward the parking area. "Chuck sends his regards, Bonnie, and wanted me to tell you he's sorry for not being able to meet you here. He's being promoted to sergeant, and the last minute details of that have to be finished today."

"Well, I'm anxious to give him my congratulations!"

"You'll get your chance for that this evening, as a matter of fact, because we're throwing him the Mother of All Parties to celebrate."

"Oooo, do I ever remember how *well* you folks *celebrate* things!"

Renee paused to look Bonnie fully in the face. "It's been much too long, my sweet love; I'm beyond words blessed to have you here with me. We've had some outrageously good times, haven't we?"

"Amen to that!"

The little group stopped beside the car, and Renee stuffed the luggage into the back of her SUV. As they were climbing in and eyeing the clouds overhead with questions of a downpour, Bonnie asked further, "And how is Bruce doing these days?"

Chuckling, "Oh, you know—it's a difficult age. He's endearing and sensitive as all get out but far too cool to ever admit it. That is, he's pretty anti-social at the present time. Ask me again in about fifteen years."

"That bad!"

"No, he's a good kid. Everybody alive has trouble maneuvering between kidhood and adulthood."

"Yes. I remember we had our share of less-

112

than-graceful days back then." Bonnie turned to look at Lucy in the back seat. "Your mom tells me you've started work on a silver Congressional Medal. I was flabbergasted to hear such a thing— that is, I'm so very impressed, honey. What do you have to do to get one of those?"

"Oh, Aunt Bonnie—it's pretty neat. You do a certain number of hours of community service (I'm helping set up and teaching beginning computers in an elementary school computer lab in an after school program), a certain number of hours of personal development—stuff in an artistic field (I'm continuing to work on the piano), a certain number of hours of a sport (I'm going to be taking tennis lessons this summer), and go on an overnight camping trip alone."

"Whew! You have an amazing amount of energy to accomplish all that! I've always thought you're one in a million, Lucy, but now I know for sure. I'm so very proud of the person you're becoming."

Renee couldn't help but add, "And after all that business, they have an award ceremony conducted by one of the U.S. senators, and—"

"You get on the six o'clock news and in the newspaper and all that sort of thing!" Lucy's enthusiasm completed her mother's thought. "But what's really cool is that it will do wonderful things for my college entrance and scholarship applications one of these days."

"You have that all planned? What do you want to do with your life?"

"Become a vet! Make animals well and happy. And for that I need to get into a good school."

113

"I wish all of us had been this focused and determined at your age!"

At this time Renee pulled into the gravel driveway of a mostly hidden bungalow, a spacious place nestled in overgrown banana and banyan trees that appeared—when it finally did appear—to be mostly open to the fragrant air. The three climbed out to stretch and exclaim over the beauties of tropical hibiscus blooms in every imaginable shade of pink and red, peach and rich lavender that strutted in profusion against arbors framing paths in three directions.

"This is just beyond description, Renee! What a fabulous gardener you are!"

"Oh gads, I don't have to do anything but stick the bushes in the ground, Bonnie; this *place* does all the rest. It ain't called paradise for nuthin'."

"Well, I'm perfectly hooked. Do you have room for me to move in with you in the next six minutes?"

"Absolutely! You can stay forever, Bonnie. My devotion to you knows no limits."

"Bless you. . . . And hey, bless me—bless all of us!"

And Bonnie felt at that very moment, God had done that in a measures too large to count. But after a week of such beatitude, it was time for Bonnie to return home to work, further recovery, and the rest of her life. It was hard to leave, yet she looked forward to even the humdrum (non-Hawaiian) parts of it as much as the high points, for it was a world view that spread spangles of joy over everything it touched.

Chapter Eleven

2003

"Hello, hello! I'm home! Mom, are you here?" Bonnie set down her suitcase beside the front door and piled her purse and keys on top of it.

"Bonnie! You're here!" Murra hurried from the kitchen, wiping her hands on a towel, to welcome her daughter home from Hawaii. "You made good time from the airport."

"Yes, but traffic was pretty heavy."

"Are you bushed?"

"I feel energized enough to wallpaper the ceilings around here; I mean, my spirits are so lifted I'm about ready to levitate."

"Well, that's just what the doctor ordered. You come sit down here and tell me all about it."

Smiling brightly, "You mean anything you haven't already heard on the phone?"

"Everything—from the beginning. And how about a cup of tea to go with it? And I just baked some snickerdoodles."

"Let me get out of these clothes, and I'm all yours."

In a few minutes Bonnie padded out to the living room on bare feet and wearing her shorty nightshirt. "Mom, I'm anxious to talk with you, but could we do it after I lie down for a little while? Now that I've stopped jerking around and can take better stock of myself, I'm realizing how bone tired I am."

114

115

"Of course that would be fine! But would you like to lie down on the sofa and let me rub your back?"

"Nothing in this life could be better than that; you're such a perfect dear."

"It's thoroughly my pleasure."

Bonnie lay down and Murra, perching on the edge, sat beside her and began kneading her back and head. "Little fuzzy growth here, Bonnie!"

"Yes, I'm starting to get back some hair. Hallelujah—I can't wait to get past the burr-cut stage." She held silent for a few minutes while the rubbing sank deep into her muscles and tried soothing the bottomless ache in the bones. But within a span of only five minutes, Bonnie was completely asleep, and it would be for hours.

"Thank you all for coming, sweet ones! This is a moment I've been looking forward to no end." Bonnie's happy face was lavish with smiles.

Her staff had grouped in her office at the end of the day for a pot luck salad supper just for the fun of being all together now that Bonnie had returned from Hawaii.

The girls (as they referred to themselves) were helping themselves to pasta and potato salads as well as a few that seemed merrily more like dessert, being based more on Cool Whip than lettuce and celery; and the talk was filled with animation and gusto. Life was good when friends could feel the blessings of fellowship.

"Was it hard to come back to reality, Bonnie?" KaNeesha wanted to know.

Beaming, "It's a little tough to give up

116

hanging out in a place that blossoms so profusely that even the tree trunks and fence posts seem to be in flower; and it was hard to leave family and old friends that I don't get to see very often—yes. But I knew that I'd be coming home to *you*, the people of my heart, and more opportunities to help patients here at work; and all that made me feel like I was merely trading one happiness for another one. As they say, 'It's all good'—every single bit of it."

"But how are you feeling?" said Kristin.

"I feel like I could take on anything." To deflect the talk away from her condition, quite unconsciously, Bonnie brightened into a little announcement. "Listen, I couldn't resist *shopping*, you know, and I'm excited to show you what I found this time." She reached for a shopping bag, one whose print was inspired by tropical florals—a little heavy on the hues of yellow and pale orange, from under her desk. "These are all for you. Just come on up here in any old order and get one of these little boxes."

Each in her turn received the small keepsake and gasped to see what rested within.

"My God, Bonnie! You are just too much. These are simply incredible," they said—with slight variations in wording—almost as one voice.

The pins were sterling silver blossoms, representative of the essence of the islands, each with a tiny cluster of diamonds at the center, and redefined friendship in a way everyone in the room felt in a profound way.

"I wanted you to know how much I was thinking of you, am always thinking of you, and that I hope you'll feel my love—without getting mushy here—whenever you see or wear these little flowers."

"Group hugs! Bonnie, group hugs!" somebody exclaimed, and they simply erupted into motion and warmth and thanksgiving for life and their dear friend Bonnie.

Later, when the last shred of spilled carrot and cherry had been scooped into the trash and everyone had gone, Bonnie still stayed a few moments longer. She dialed a long familiar number to her bone specialist, Dr. Cliffton.

"Hello, Ron? This is Bonnie."

"Great to hear from you! How was your trip to paradise?"

"Fabulous—really and truly—and always worthy of the name."

"Hey, I want to thank you for the birthday card, kiddo. It was completely nuts! Didn't think I'd ever stop laughing!"

"My pleasure. You're so much fun to tease."

"Well, what can I do for you, Bonnie? I'm wondering if you're having increasing bone problems since you're calling at such an unusual hour."

"I don't know if it's the same osteoarthritis I've had forever or something new, Ron, but it just *aches* so that I can hardly stand it. Is there something more I could be taking for the pain?"

"Yes, but Bonnie, you need to get some tests run over there—I mean cancer tests in case we *are* dealing with something new here."

"Oh sure, I will. But since I stopped the

118

chemo, I've been feeling wonderful—well, except for the pain and being tired all the time. I don't think Dr. Menier would've taken me off the treatments if he thought I needed more."

"I'm not sure how to interpret that, Bonnie. . . . I'll certainly prescribe something more for you, but please get some additional tests."

"I will. I promise."

"Let me know how this new stuff works."

"Okay, you've got it."

Two months later Bonnie had come home from work and had lain down right away while her mother continued the usual loving back rubs that had become their evening custom.

Just now she was stirring awake. Once Bonnie was sitting up, she ran a hand across her eyes, then her head.

"Hi, sweet curly top!" Murra said with a laugh.

"Mmmm—am I awake? What did you say?—curly top?" Pausing, "Can you believe my hair came back like this, Mom? I've wanted to have curly hair all my life!"

"I know that!"

"It must be a sign that I'm getting better."

"Well, I'm sure I've never seen you look so beautiful and vibrant. How do you *feel*?"

"Spectacular. Maybe a little tired."

"Do you feel up to talking about what your cancer doctor had to say in your appointment today?"

"Same old, same old. But he did put me on some new meds. I'm sure these will do me a

119

lot of good; I'll be well in no time. And you know I've been taking the new ones from Ron Cliffton, my bone guy." She stopped talking to allow a brief spell of coughing.

As a bit of a stall maneuver, Murra poured more tea for both of them, wondering if she should bring up the alarming phone call she had received that day. *"How completely distressing to find that the doctor had not given her a clean bill of health when taking her off the chemo treatments after all. With so much cancer riddled all through her bones now—especially, he said, her ribs—he thinks operating would be pointless if not impossible and wanted to know if I would be willing, along with other people in the family, to see if we would match for a bone marrow transplant. Why hasn't she told me about this! Does Bonnie know that her doctor called me? Should I bring it up? . . . Maybe not; we have so little time together to spoil it with unwelcome topics unless she decides to tell me herself."*

"Mom? Are you okay? You look so sad all of a sudden."

"Well, I just don't like to see you so tired all the time. Maybe, as you say, the new meds will clear things up."

"I'm very hopeful. Really. I've been doing a lot of research online about cancer treatments and new drugs and findings. It's amazing how much can be done these days compared with a decade ago. I mean, hey—it's a new millennium; that has to count for something." She reached for her tea cup but found picking it up was an unsteady proposition.

120

"What is it, Bonnie?"

"Nothing much. My fingers—um, I guess my feet as well—are sort of tingling. It's weird, but I'm sure it's not anything that can't be explained by the new medication." After another fit of coughing, she smiled weakly and said, "Maybe I'll just go to bed. Maybe that's the ticket. I'm positive I'll feel better in the morning."

"Do you have to go in to work tomorrow? Maybe you're trying to do too much."

"No! I'm fine! And we have a staff meeting set up for 11:00 that I need to attend; I just can't let this new project get started without making sure each of my girls knows exactly what she can do to succeed in her individual part."

Not arguing, "I know how much they depend on your judgment and organization."

"I can't let them down."

"Would you like a brownie before you go to bed?"

"No, Mom, thanks. I'm fine." She headed for the bedroom without more discussion.

Alone, Murra stacked the cups and teapot along with the plate of brownies on a tray and carried them into the kitchen. *Oh my Lord God, I don't know how to pray for this any more. It's coming to the point—I feel very strongly— that only a miracle will save her. I pray for that miracle with all my heart and soul.* Murra wiped her eyes. *"Only You know Your own plan for her life, but if a miracle would be within Your will, please heal Bonnie, Lord. Please bring my little girl into remission."*

When witches and skulls and other symbols of

death adorn doorways, then everyone recognizes the last half of October has come to propose its special type of seasonal wisdom (or lack of it). Bonnie had always found it odd that society would celebrate evil and damnation so gleefully—as if life itself didn't offer enough issues to cause fear without asking for more—but just now she was mostly ignoring the orange and black decorations as she strode down the hall to Dr. Menier's office for the results of her most recent battery of tests.

She felt, as the saying goes, like a million bucks with her curly hair, chunky gold earrings, and new wool blazer, the latter two having been birthday presents from her mother two months ago and now finally seeing temperatures slightly cooler enough to wear.

Here was the doctor's door on the second floor, and Bonnie swept up to it with a smile as wide as the opening. She was sure the news would be an improvement and upturn in her health, and her chipper knock announced that very notion.

Dr. Menier was standing in front of the wall of windows on the far side, one arm folded and propping the elbow of his other one; lightly his finger and thumb stroked absently along his jaw line—a man deep in thought.

"Hello, hello!" Bonnie spouted from the door.

The man startled. Apparently he hadn't heard the knock. "Ah. Bonnie. You're right on time."

Abruptly, the moment seemed to slice off from the river of time and froze. It seemed al-

122

most as a physical iceberg to be stopped, examined and handled, and even more, *remembered*.

"Brad, are you okay? You look like one of the ghosts on the doors out there took form and started flying around in here. What is it?"

He cleared his throat. "Bonnie, have a seat." His eyes never left the floor, and his voice managed hardly more than a rasp.

"You're scaring me, Brad; what is it?"

He came around his desk and sat in the chair beside her. "Bonnie, there's no easy way to say this—"

She grabbed his hand. "Brad, are you sick? Is something wrong? I mean, do you have cancer yourself or—"

"No, I would welcome it gladly if I could trade it for my next sentence."

Softly, "Then it's better to spit it out, and let's look at it."

"Yes. Your tests have come back, and Bonnie, I'm afraid it's not good news. The cancer is so very advanced; you have only two and a half months to live."

All the color drained from her face as her heart seemed to flip over in her chest. "Two and a half months?" Her tone raked across gravel, aghast.

"I'm so sad about this, my friend, that I can hardly breathe. I really thought we were going to crush this, but we got such a late start with the treatments that—"

She seized his other hand as well. "Brad, oh listen—it's not your fault! You've been a prince! You've done everything humanly possible to help me every single step of the way."

123

"It shouldn't have happened!" He wiped his eyes.

With more than gentleness, "It had spread by the time we became aware of it. You know—dare I say it?—I wasn't being very well monitored. You *tried;* you have to believe that this isn't your fault."

"I'm so sorry, Bonnie. . . . My medical advice at this point is to get even busier than you already are to *live*—go on every trip you've ever dreamed of and make every minute count. If you want to travel—do it! If you want to keep working here—do it! The world is your oyster."

"If I want to dig for pearls? Will I be strong enough?"

"Up until the end, yes—I think so."

For a moment her face went completely blank. Then she stood up and, regaining her usual composure, said, "I feel a yammering fit coming on; think I'd better aim it into my office."

"Sure, that's fine. I'll come down in a little while to see how you're doing."

Bonnie did aim her response into the privacy of her own four walls. After drawing the blinds across the wall of windows opening on the front courtyard gardens, she wept from one end of her life to the other, and how the snapshots of her years flashed and flickered in her mind's eye. She sat at her desk but turned her back to the door, and nobody disturbed her.

"I thought I was fighting it with every ounce of strength and gumption I had. Really believed I would conquer it—really believed!

124

This seems impossible: I look healthy as a horse, a curly one! And what on earth is this going to do to Mom?"

She hugged her arms around herself. *"I need a plan for the next couple of months. Trips, friends, activity, and little time to think about what's really happening. That sounds like something workable: a cheat on reality. But what to do about my staff?"*

Bonnie straightened up and dried her eyes and face. She forced herself to breathe deeply and walked across to the side table to brew a fresh pot, a necessary item in the play out of the next scene. Then she buzzed all eight of her girls over the intercom.

Once they were assembled and each had a cup of the coffee, Bonnie took a spot before them leaning against the front of her desk.

"I hardly know how to say this. . . . Guess I'll just jump right in. I've had some bad news on my cancer update this morning, and it appears we're going to need my job to be understandable to all of you so the work of the office can go on when I'm not here."

"BONNIE! What are you saying!"

"I'm not sure how long I'll be able to work, guys; that's all." Did she tell them about the two and a half months' time frame? No. Had she already come to disbelieve it herself? Possibly.

Everyone began talking at once. More questions than Bonnie could or felt like answering peppered the air. But at last she had to say, "Listen, sweet ones, I need to get home. It's been too much of a day. I'm sure you understand."

In shock, of course they all did. And after

Bonnie left, the eight of them stayed and could talk of nothing else.

"She looks so healthy and fit."

"Yes, my God!—you wouldn't even know she's been sick."

"She's always in such a kind and upbeat mood."

"How can this possibly be happening?"

Bonnie had been home only a few minutes when Dr. Cliffton, her bone specialist and long-time friend, stopped by after his consultation with Dr. Menier. In effect, he had all but followed her there from the cancer center. They had been sitting down and begun talking about the devastating news when Murra came in from shopping.

"Why Ron Cliffton! What a surprise to see you," she exclaimed at once, setting down her bags and parcels. The lilt in her voice said she was enjoying a jubilant mood. To her mind, seeing how lovely and filled with good color and health her daughter appeared topped the list of reasons for happiness. "It's been a long time. How are you, anyway?" she chirped.

But abruptly, when Murra happened to glimpse Bonnie's face, she noticed the snuffed look that recent tears had left in her eyes; and her mind froze. Something in this scene was terribly wrong. "What's happening?" she murmured.

"I was just getting Ron something to drink, Mom. Would you like something too?" Bonnie was up in a second, anything to divert attention from the inevitable telling of the truth.

126

"Yes. Here, I'll help you."

The three went into the kitchen where Murra, taking charge of the provisions, began setting out glasses for iced tea or soda.

"Tea is fine," said the doctor.

"I'll have some ginger ale, Mom. Thanks. And thanks for taking care of it."

The tension in the air seemed to lather around them. Murra handed them the drinks and reached for her own. Suddenly Bonnie's weak and unsteady hand jerked out from under her glass, and the full twelve ounces dumped all over the counter, between the cupboard and refrigerator and even into the floor space behind. Bonnie jumped back with stress and a hand thrown over her heart.

"Oh! How klutzy of me! Can't seem to corral these spazzy hands today."

"Never mind, dear. I'll get it mopped up in no time. Why don't you both go sit down; I'll be right with you."

While the two wandered back into the living room, Murra slid into action with towels and a long handled mop. Yet her mind was far from the scene of the trivial spill. *"Lord, please help us here. I don't know what's going on, but I'm* afraid, *Father, more afraid than I can ever remember. Please be with us and bring us Your peace."* At last Murra was finished and followed the others out of the kitchen.

When she finally sat down, her eyes were drawn to Dr. Cliffton.

"Mrs. Kenneford, I'm afraid there's some distressing news about Bonnie's condition—the results of those most recent tests. Since I'm here,

Bonnie has asked me to be the one to tell you." He went on to explain because Bonnie had no way to say such unthinkable words to her mother, especially when she wasn't sure she believed them herself.

"Two and a half *months?*" Murra faltered as soon as she heard. "How can this be?" Immediately the numbness that clutched her throat felt all-consuming, and it spread upward to all parts of her brain. Words wouldn't come. Tears were dammed at the source. Adrenaline flooded her body with fear. But outwardly she appeared surprisingly calm.

"Thank you so much for driving out here, Dr. Cliffton," she managed at last. "We certainly appreciate it."

He might have stayed in a supportive fatherly role for a while longer, but he understood the needs of the moment and rose at once. "It was my pleasure," he said stiffly. "Bonnie, you must call me if you need anything large or small, any time of the day or night. Promise me."

Softly, "I promise."

And in a moment, he was gone. The two stood on the porch, watching as he pulled out of the driveway and headed off down the street.

"Are you okay, Mom?" Bonnie asked with concern when the spell was broken.

Simply, "I have no way to see how this is possible. You look absolutely beautiful and vibrant and young! How can you be so sick that you're—"

"I know the feeling; I see it that way too," Bonnie interrupted specifically to avoid having the "d" word loosed upon the air. "But listen—

128

Dr. Menier actually told me to get busy with the time I have left and *party hearty,* beginning now and lasting till the end of the year; and that's what I intend for us to do. Where would you like to go first?"

"Go? Bonnie, this doesn't make any sense! If you feel well enough to be going places, how can you be—"

"How about a little jaunt to Catalina Island? We haven't been out there in twenty-odd years. I can make all the arrangements, and maybe we can go next week. And if I ask Ed and Grace to join us, it would be just that much more special." Her brother and his wife, who lived in Canada, had not been this far south for years.

The boat out to Catalina Island, leaving from the port of Los Angeles at San Pedro, was a speedy new one with high drama and spray that set the mood for a glistening afternoon. Once they had zipped the twenty miles across the bay and disembarked, Bonnie and Murra along with Ed and Grace took a taxi to their hotel. Their special older but charming place sat high on the hill overlooking the deep turquoise blue of Avalon Bay, a myriad of small pleasure boats, and fringy palms punctuating the scene. The surrounding hills themselves appeared dry and dotted with sparse chaparral and yucca in exactly the same way the foothills did throughout the whole southern California coastal area.

"Woo-hoo!" whooped Ed when they had settled their suitcases in the rooms. "Our northwest conifer forest this is not! What a great view we have here! Just look at the color of that water."

"It's glorious, isn't it?" said Bonnie at once. "And you *guys*—I'm just so *thrilled* you could get away to join us here. What an incredible treat!"

Grace was just returning from the pop machine with cans of coke for each of them. "Listen, we need to get out there and *explore*," she exclaimed as she shut the door with one bare foot.

"On the way up the hill I saw a sign for some self-driven carts for tours," said Murra.

Ed laughed and rolled his eyes. "Self-driven! That sounds better than anything they could offer."

"But should we trust your wild ways behind the wheel?"

"Aw, shucks, Mom," he drawled for effect.

Murra basked in the sweetness of having two of her children with her at the same time, not a frequent event. "Do you want to rest a little while first, Bonnie?"

"Yes, I think I might be better off lying down for a few minutes. Maybe you three could go rent the cart and come back here for me?"

"Sounds like a perfect plan. You'll be okay here by yourself?"

"Sure as shootin'. . . as they used to say around these here parts."

"They did?" Grace smiled her puzzlement.

"Evidently they used to shoot some of the old western movies here on the island for the sake of the wild buffalo herd and the even wilder western scenery."

"How cool; I didn't know that. Will we see

130

some of these famous beasts today?"

With a straight face, "We will not sleep tonight until we've patted at least three bison noses."

"Gotcha!"

In a few minutes Bonnie had curled up on one of the beds and the three left, walking, for the electric cart rental booth down the hill. And within a half hour the small pink conveyance had brought them back up to collect their missing passenger. Then it was time to set out on an adventure.

Rural roads led all over the island. Sometimes these visitors were offered spectacular panoramas of the rugged coastline; other views centered on dense brush woodlands with steep embankments or rough canyons within the interior. But wherever they went—and making bad turns became the uproarious order of the day—the spirits were sizzling.

"Whoa! Stop!" Bonnie laughed. "I need to sit in back where the gullet of the road isn't trying to swallow me whole on some of these two wheeled turns of yours!"

"Hey—wait a minute little sister! You aren't insulting my driving, are you?"

"Who me? Not me!" She popped to a standing position as soon as Ed stopped the cart. "Here, Mom, why don't you trade places with me? It'll give you a chance to catch up on your son's presence in a *really* up close and personal way. Be my guest."

Laughing, Murra exchanged seats with her, and the little band of travelers moved on once more.

131

"Good grief—would you look at *that!*" Grace suddenly cheered. "Up there. Above the treetops!"

They all cast their vision where she was pointing so urgently, and how their sight was filled. The wing spans on the two wheeling birds seemed all but infinite.

"What are they?—bald eagles?"

"Yes, I think so; they have to be! I think they have some kind of sanctuary for them on the island."

"Can you imagine? Here in the *wild* just a stone's throw from one of the world's most populated cities? Incredible." Bonnie's voice held low. "This is a view I'll treasure for the rest of my life. . . . Um, guess I'd better hurry up and treasure the living daylights out of it before I run out of time!" She tried to make a joke out of her little slip of the tongue; and because she was smiling so brilliantly and having such fun, nobody scuffed against the mood enough to be sad—at least out loud.

"Looks like we're coming up on an historical marker, folks," Ed informed them as they rounded a bend. He yanked to a stop, and everybody bucked forward. "Oops, sorry about that!" With a good natured chuckle, he climbed out and helped each of the ladies. "An archaeological site going back nearly 7,000 years," he continued when they had all grouped around the display.

"Imagine old time-y native folks living here before the age of neon made the mainland sparkle almost in their laps." Grace sounded almost solemn. "What would they think now if they could come back and see the changes?"

Bonnie's smile was thoughtful. "I'd bet they'd think we dress funny, and I'm not sure they'd be all that impressed with our 'progress.'"

"Well, except in medicine," Murra said quickly. Then she regretted her words as silently each considered how medical progress was currently failing their Bonnie.

But it was Bonnie herself who rescued the mood. "Oh look, Mom—the little animal over there. What is it? A fox?

"Yes! I think so—there, slinking behind that rock?"

Grace took up the rescue as well. "One of the rarest of God's critters out here on the island. I'll bet its particular kind lives nowhere else on earth."

"Absolutely," said Murra as she rested a hand on her daughter-in-law's shoulder. "God takes special care of everything—and everyone, even when all else fails."

"Hey—I'll drink to that!" Ed pulled bottled water out of the little cooler built into the cart. "I suspect we all will."

Everyone appreciated the cool break as much as a lightening of the mood. "This hits the spot," said Bonnie, "but what about our buffalo?"

"Looks, like we'll have to drive around a little more."

They headed the little vehicle even farther toward the interior and had sliced around many more quick turns before reaching an area of grassy hillsides where, as advertised, dozens upon dozens of the shaggy beasts dotted the scene like variously sized boulders against the brush. And as the sun started slipping toward its dip into the sea along the back coast of the island, they found several mothers and babies along with some others who were beside the roadside rather than across a field.

"Does anybody want to get close enough to pat them?" Murra wondered. "I'm not sure I do, for one."

"Well, we've come all this way . . ." Bonnie said with a smile. "Is anybody with me?"

"Heck, I'll do it, Bonnie." Ed climbed out, then reached a hand to help her. "It'll be just like old times—making Mom count her reasons for going gray!"

The two, holding one another around the waist, ventured beyond the pavement toward the little buffalo group.

Whispering, Ed leaned closer to his sister's ear. "Maybe we'd better go for a single adult and not a mama protecting her baby—in case they're anything like bears and might feel like eating us for dinner."

"Yes, and maybe we'd better aim our pats at the rump rather than the nose, seeing as how that's pretty darn close to the jaw."

They inched closer, pretending to be perfectly relaxed. Having located the one animal who fit their criteria (single adult, prominent rump), they fixed their sight there and moved in. And quite casually, with the utmost gentleness, both laid a soft touch on the backside and then turned to hightail it out of there.

"Eeee-haw!" whooped Bonnie once they were safely back in the cart. "That was just the best! Did you see us, Mom?"

134

Laughing so that her eyes watered, Murra could only shake her head and seal up the wonderful memory for later, forever. "Yes, dear, I saw you!"

Now the twilight began drawing down, and the group decided on dinner as the next step in their special day. Still, since Bonnie was particularly tired, she wanted to lie down while the others brought her a little something to eat after their meal. And while Ed and Grace attended a night club floor show, Murra returned to their rooms to rub Bonnie's back and tuck her into bed for the night.

"It was a fabulous day, wasn't it, Mom?"

"It could not have been better. This was an amazing idea, Bonnie. I'm glad you insisted."

After breakfast the next morning, the group decided to visit all the shops clustered along the streets of the crescent-shaped bay in the quaint town of Avalon. Looking for nothing in particular but fascinated to see whatever wares were being offered, they strolled through one after another of the tiny stores, most of them family owned, at a leisurely pace for most of the morning and afternoon.

"Look—how cool is that!" Bonnie said, pointing to several human street sweepers taking fussy care of the pristine cleanliness of the place.

"Unforgettable, just like the little shops," Murra smiled.

The Perico Gallery became a favorite for their watercolor prints and pen and ink drawings while the uniquely titled boutique Buoys

135

and Gulls Sportswear provided a place for Catalina Island souvenir T-shirts and hats. But at last, once the gift purchases were accomplished and the rampant creativity of the crafts enjoyed, the group decided on an early dinner to talk over old times and the current day.

"What are we in the mood to eat? Italian? Mexican? Seafood? Steak?" Ed asked.

"All of the above!" the other three cried almost at once.

After selecting an acclaimed waterfront steak house (with a vast and varied menu), the four made their way to the upstairs dining room where high vaulting windows insisted on glorious harbor vistas framed by palm trees in the foreground.

"Spectacular," Bonnie breathed as she selected a seat facing all this visual wealth.

"Isn't it, though?" said Murra, settling beside her.

Ed and Grace filled in the other two seats, and at once Ed had caught the attention of a server. "Margaritas all around!" he exclaimed. "Did I remember what everybody likes?"

They all agreed completely.

Along with the drinks came a special welcome for early guests from a strolling singer with his guitar. "We're pleased to have you join us this evening," he said. "Call me Pedro, and make your requests. I will sing for you anything!"

"Do you have a special favorite, Bonnie?" her brother asked.

"Oh absolutely—'Love Me Tender' is always at the top of my list."

The musician smiled broadly, revealing

136

straight, bright teeth against bronzed skin. "Ah, you make the evening start with love and magic, truly." Closing his eyes with a dreamy cast, he began in a sultry baritone, "'Love me tender, Love me sweet, Never let me go. You have made my life complete, And I love you so. . . . Love me tender, Love me true, All my dreams. . . .'"

"My life *is* complete" Bonnie said in almost a whisper as the lyrics sank into each of them and eventually the song itself faded away. She paused to gather all their eyes. "I hope everyone alive comes to the point of feeling this way. I *still believe* I'm going to have more of life than the doctors give me; but in spite of everything, all told I've had every fulfillment a person could want."

"Do you have a particular word for it, sis?" Ed gazed at her with attention.

"Yes! I believe it's *peace*. The sense that whatever happens, I'm going to somehow claw my way above it and be there tranquilly doing the best I can."

"Gee, Bonnie, that's so beautiful," said Grace.

"Well, it's not any kind of biggy Manifesto or Philosophy of Life, nothing to get too excited about. It's more of a sense of calm."

"God, how many people really *feel* that way!"

"What does it, Bonnie?" Ed asked. "Is it a lack of selfish ambition and more a giving of the self to the benefit of others?—because that's the way it's always struck me that you live."

"Y'all're gonna make me blush," she quipped.

"No, seriously: that strikes me as your legacy to all of us, a sort of model of how we can be happy. That's no small feat."

"Come on, now, broth.; I don't do 'feats.' I's jus' me."

"Okay, okay, I'll cut out the mush. But we do love you so very much."

Murra wiped at the corners of her eyes and took a gulp of her drink while Bonnie smiled her appreciation for the kindest words she had ever imagined. "Another song!" she cried to cover the inevitable bit of embarrassment she felt.

"Yellow Submarine!" hooted Grace, instinctively wanting to help lighten the mood.

"Where'd you get that, honey?" Ed leaned his arm around behind her.

"We're staring at boats! What could be better? . . . Do you know that song?" she asked the musician.

"Oh yes, I can do that one." And so he began, "'In the town where I was born, Lived a man who sailed to sea, And he told us of his life, In the land of submarines . . . .'" When he came to the chorus, everyone at the table chimed in to sing along—with clapping.

"'We all live in a yellow submarine, yellow submarine, yellow submarine. . . .'"

And by the second chorus, the whole room—though not completely filled at this earlier hour—couldn't help but join in as well. "'Every one of us has all we need, Sky of blue, and sea of green, In our yellow submarine. . . .'"

And Bonnie couldn't help but underscore the theme, "Indeed we do have all we need. Why, people, we all *do* live in a yellow submarine!"

Ed and Grace were able to stay at Bonnie's house

138

for a short while longer after the group's return from Catalina Island. To celebrate life properly in these circumstances, a sort of reunion luncheon rose as a most satisfying idea.

"We could invite absolutely *everybody* and have it out on the patio," Bonnie suggested. "And maybe we could ask Kristin, my artist friend from work, to bring some of her canvases to display—hopefully sell!—at the same time. I've been wanting to do that for her, and this seems like a cool time, don't you think?"

"If it wouldn't make you too tired, Bonnie," her mother said at once. "That's the most important consideration in my view."

"Well, I could rest now and then if the necessity arose."

"Yes, and you'd have to let us do absolutely all the preparations."

Smiling broadly, "I'll give you no argument there! You know how much I love to cook!"

Grace jumped into the discussion. "Well, you could sit perfectly still and watch cute little sandwiches and salads spring up before your eyes from our busy hands. It'll be fun."

"And I know eight girls from work who would be insulted if they didn't each get to bring a dessert." Bonnie hugged her arms around herself with contentment. "How soon can we get all this organized?"

"As long as it takes to make phone calls and scoot to the market." Murra said. "How about Saturday? That will give us three days."

"That sounds fine to me," Grace agreed.

Eagerness filled Bonnie's eyes. "And at this time of year, just the end of October, people won't be all booked up—except for the 31st, of course. We'll probably find people available more right now than at any other time during the fall."

Murra's depth of sadness overturned her expression, but it was only for an instant while she worked at hiding it behind something less revealing. Her words were soft but guarded, "Well, Bonnie, I believe they'd all come to see *you* no matter what time of the year it happened to be." She did not mention their need to say goodbye to this special friend while they still had the chance, but the unspoken thought hung in the air heavily.

"What kinds of salads shall we have?" Grace's diversion came as almost a pounce to lighten the mood.

"People would be pleased from pea to potato," Bonnie quipped. "Think I'll go make a few of those calls and maybe lie down for a little while."

"That sounds fine," said Murra. "The three of us will head for the grocery store and get things in gear."

Bonnie had insisted on having the customary large scare crow and hay bale sitting on the front porch as a welcome to these harvest-time guests. Actually, it was Scare-Bear, a huge teddy dressed in flannel shirt and jeans with a straw hat and strands of straw sticking out of random spots on his attire. Gold and brown balloons also marked the house by bobbing in the breeze from the overhang on the porch roof.

Still, the place wasn't hard to find, for

140

everybody on the list had visited here many times for the little patio parties Bonnie had loved to host through the years. But this one was to be different; according to Bonnie's doctors, this would be the last.

With balmy warmth and more green than October normally allows—except in fortunate spots like southern California and Florida—the patio was packed with everyone-all-at-once and ringed by Kristin Bennet's bright oil paintings. Champagne was flowing freely, and many a small toast—in addition to the formal one made by Ed to Bonnie's health—was actually a silent prayer for her well being and a thoroughly considered thanksgiving for the part she had played in each of these lives.

"Bonnie, you look fabulous," her dear friend Angelina was saying after a sip of her first margarita. "I insist that you understand this truth."

"Watch out, or you'll make me blush."

"Well, the curly locks on top of your head make you look like a young starlet."

"Oh, *please*," she said, rolling her eyes, "Angelina, you're too much."

"Nope, I won't let you talk me out of it: I calls 'em as I sees 'em."

"Okay, then, . . . your kind and majestically truthful words have made my day!"

Laughing, "You go girl!"

"Did you get enough to eat? There's plenty over there. Be sure you try the chocolate cheese cake my co-worker Doris made."

Patting her hips, "Yeah, just what I need is an extra slice of that settling *right here!* Have you had anything yourself, Bonnie?"

"I'm not all that hungry, Ange. Honestly." Bonnie took a sip of the water she had in a champagne flute and smiled across at a nearby group of friends.

"Bonnie! Angelina! Come join us." The subject at hand held a strict sort of lightness. "We're just deciding whether we can believe that Scott Peterson guy accused of killing his wife, Lacy, and their unborn son. Have you been following the case?" The speaker, Marlene, was one of Bonnie's oldest friends.

"Oh yes, absolutely; it's been riveting learning all the details." Still, Bonnie secretly wondered how long she could keep standing upright with the deep pain in her bones.

"So do you think he's guilty?"

"From everything I've heard, I can only think yes. But you just know it'll be another year before he goes to trial, with the way things grind along under the wheels of justice—except on *Law and Order,* of course, where everything gets wrapped up nicely in an hour—or two at the max."

"No kidding. . . . Well, I have to say, you're certainly looking good, Bonnie."

"Isn't she, though?" piped Angelina. "I was just trying to convince her of that indisputable little fact."

Blushing slightly, "Thank you; it really makes me feel wonderful to hear you say it. But listen, Marlene—I've been reading about all the wonderful work you've been doing at the teen center outside of town."

"Oh gosh, thank you. The migrant worker

142

problem isn't just one touching adults—but don't get me started on all the needs!"

Bonnie smiled. "We're very proud of you, sweet one."

The afternoon moved by at a pace too quickly for people with mortality on their minds but with no way to express it outwardly in words. Certainly Bonnie didn't look sick at all, let alone sick enough to be dying before the end of the year; but how do individuals deal with such knowledge while observing social graces? How do we keep ourselves from sweeping the beloved dying friend into our arms and weeping from our soul upward—even with primitive, instinctive wails over the injustice of life and the steadfastness of our love—while civilized functions seem to require decorum and proper restraint? We want to be true and real, even sloppy with kisses and huggings; but are such outpourings socially acceptable? And how hard is it for the person standing on the brink to hear such wrenchings of the spirit, anyway?

As all the guests left the party, they did hug Bonnie goodbye, and most managed it without large displays of tears. Still, the smiles and bright, upbeat wishes were deeply moving and sincere even without the deeper yearnings to connect.

Bonnie's smiles in return were only radiant, the one gift she could give them, a memory for quiet moments in their future years.

Once everyone had left with their final goodbyes, Bonnie paused in the entry hall with her arms folded around herself and with her mother, brother, and sister-in-law standing there beside her.

"That was just the best," she murmured.

Murra gave her a quick hug as Ed and Grace headed out to the patio to start the process of cleanup. "I thought so too, Bonnie. Everyone loves you very much. I'm so glad they all were able to stop by."

"Mom, would you mind terribly if I got my hot Epsom salts bath now? I don't think I've ever been this tired—and with a headache, really intense backache, you name it."

"I've been worried that would be the effect on you of such a big affair this afternoon."

"Did it show?"

"Heavens no! You were wonderful—perky, congenial, the best hostess in the world, dear. It's always so hard to remember how horrible you feel because you ignore it or cover it over so well."

"Thanks, Mom. I needed to hear that."

"Is there anything I can do to help you feel more comfortable?"

"Maybe a backrub when I get finished with my bath?"

"It will be my pleasure, as ever. Maybe you could get in bed while I do that so if you fall asleep, you won't have to leave the sofa to relocate for the night."

"That sounds like pure heaven to me."

The next day Ed and Grace left for their return trip to Canada. And the day after that Bonnie's other brother, Gene, and his wife, Charlene, flew in from Wichita, Kansas with their two children

144

for a last visit.

"Aunt Bonnie! Aloha!" exclaimed Jillian, settling a slightly lopsided lei of lavender mums around her beloved aunt's neck by means of standing on her tiptoes.

"What have you done, child? Did you make this for me?"

Beaming, "Yes. Mommy said chrysanthemums are the only good flowers we have in Kansas right now, so I had to make it out of those instead of lilies or orchids or something cool like we had in Hawaii."

"Well, these are completely beautiful, little love. Thank you and aloha to you too." Bonnie hugged her dear niece and then turned to the younger brother. "This tall person can't possibly be Taylor, can it?"

With a sudden bolt of shyness, "Yes. . . . Aunt Bonnie, I made this for you too!" He handed her a crayon drawing of unusually well-formed monsters in rainbow hues. "It's some of the characters in that book you always read to me when you were at our house."

"Oh—they're from *Where the Wild Things Are.* I certainly remember that one and how we always laughed at the wonderful pictures. These are very handsome wild things, Taylor—thank you. Would you all like to come with me to the kitchen while I hang this fine picture on the refrigerator?"

The two children, ages ten and eight, both slipped their hands around Bonnie's elbows and skipped beside her into the kitchen. Meanwhile, the parents were still settling their suitcases inside the door while Murra greeted them with

145

hugs and exclamations of happiness to see them here.

Before long everyone had found a place in the living room with some cider as the welcoming liquid. The chat and reminiscence was spirited, for it had been a good while since they had all been together.

"Aunt Bonnie, we saw a swimming pool down the street with kids playing in it," Jillian pointed out during the pause in conversation she had been waiting for. "At home in Kansas we've already had frost, and here you lucky ducks get to hang out at the pool!"

"Well, would you two like to be that lucky and go for a swim?" said Bonnie with a smile. "That pool belongs to our Home Owners Association, and you're perfectly welcome to hang out there with the other kids if that would make you happy."

"We wouldn't want to be any trouble," piped Charlene.

"Oh, heavens no! I'd dive in myself," she said with a laugh, "if I weren't so interested in keeping my hair nice for 'company'—that is, you guys!"

"Well, it does look great, Bonnie," said her brother. "So curly! It didn't used to be curly, did it?"

"No, it never was. See the interesting benefits of exotic medications?"

Jillian had started to bounce with anticipation. And right away Murra rose to collect the glasses to carry into the kitchen. "How about if the kids have a swim and then we all go somewhere nice for lunch? The Palm Springs area has

146

anything we could ever want."

"That sounds great, Mom," Charlene said. "I can't wait to try something unusual. . . . Here, Let me help you with those."

The table at the Outback Steakhouse in Palm Desert was ample for the four adults and two wet-haired children as they settled in for a late lunch overlooking the festive patio.

Almost at once the servers had brought a pitcher of something they called the "Down Under 'Rita," margaritas with an Australian flair, and a huge deep fried "Bloomin' Onion" appetizer for all to sample and splurge upon.

"It looks like a sunburst, doesn't it?" Bonnie observed while the others pulled off the beams closest to them and visited the dipping sauce with their morsels.

"Fitting for this part of the world," said Charlene. "Sunshine 100% of the time and, it seems like, twenty-four hours a day. What a great place to live!"

"I feel that way—it really *is* fun living here. No snow to shovel or ice to drive on. No worry about changing plans on account of the weather."

"I think the sunburst idea describes you, Bonnie, even better than the southern California desert." Gene held up his drink as a sort of toast to his sister.

"Me?"

"Yes. No matter what high wind or nastiness is going on all around, you're there with your sunny smile and encouraging words with all the sizzle of a beaming star—or sun, in our case here on earth. . . . Here's to you, sis: the sunshine in all our lives."

"To Bonnie!" They all clinked glasses.

"Good grief, Gene!" she said at once. "What kind words! But how do I sit here and listen to them without all shades of embarrassment?"

A long pause. "Well, Bonn, you know—we all really have to take some time to say what we think and how we feel before it's too late. *Everybody's* life is incredibly short; *nobody* is guaranteed years stretching into forever; and if we don't get our deepest thoughts made known when we have the chance—no matter how awkward it may be to tell those things—then chances are they won't get communicated at all. It's the same for everybody alive, I think."

Bonnie looked at the ice cubes in the water glass she was holding and said softly, "I was going to protest that I'm not sure the doctors are right about how much time I have; I'm not willing to accept it, not even a little. I'm still fighting, by golly. But instead I have to say that you're absolutely right: that's true for anyone, anywhere. . . . Still, it's hard to hear such amazingly beautiful sentiments, but you have to know it means the world to me that you decided to share them."

But the moment was punctuated with a small sniff at Bonnie's side. She paused to see what it meant. "Taylor, are you all right, honey?"

The child wiped his eyes with the back of his fist. "Aunt Bonnie, I don't want you to die!" he blurted softly.

She leaned a bit to reach him for a hug.

"Well, sweet one, I don't want to die right now either. I hope I won't. We have many, many more stories we need to read together and things we need to laugh about. We'll keep a happy thought that we'll get the chance."

"That's a good way to leave it," said Murra with hope. "We'll have faith that God's in control and has a plan that's taking care of everything happening to us—whatever it may turn out to be."

"Does that mean you've stopped praying for a miracle, Mom?"

"Heavens no! But I also know that miracles come in all shapes and sizes."

"What do you mean, exactly?" Gene asked.

"Well, God promises that no matter what happens, it's working for our good, our benefit, in the long run. Sometimes things seem tragic and negative at the time; but in every case, years later you can look back and see how perfect the answer He gave actually was. His promise is that *all things* work together *for good,* and I cling to that every day of my life. Without that particular faith, I don't see how we can make sense of all the awful things that happen to us."

"So you believe in having faith in the big picture that may not be visible to us at a given time?" Leaning forward, Charlene set down her glass.

"Yes, that's exactly right."

"Well, listen," Bonnie said at last, "having life at all—and family, friends, a home, peacefulness—is pretty miraculous itself when you get right down to it. I say we make our toast to *that.*"

"Yes, to life!"

"To the miracle of life itself!"

When the visit was finished and the day arrived for Gene and his family to fly back to Kansas, the ideas of its being possibly their last time together, of sunbursts, miracles both seen and currently unseen, of faith and love and laughter—all these floated in the air around them as they said their goodbyes. Negatives and positives were kept in balance by faith: these helped them manage to get through the scene without breaking down in tears.

"Goodbye, Aunt Bonnie. I love you."

"Aunt Bonnie, here's a little bear I brought from Kansas for you—it's for love and for cheering you up when you're down." Jillian's token smiled with winsome eyes almost buried in fluffy pink fur. "Bye, Aunt Bonnie. You're the best."

She hugged both children at once. "I love you more than you could ever know. . . . And Gene, Char—have a safe trip, and take care."

Chapter Twelve

2003

"Oh Mom, I can't begin to tell you how wonderful that feels and how much I love you for taking such good care of me." The backrub was particularly soothing this late afternoon because, after all the house guests and trips, Bonnie was suffering a great deal of pain.

"I wish I could do more, Bonnie. Believe me when I tell you how frustrated I feel at not being able to take away the bad things altogether."

"You're more comfort than anyone could imagine." Bonnie sat up and turned so she could see her mother's face. "You know how hard it is for me to lean on people, Mom, but one thing this illness has taught me is that it's *okay* to lean sometimes. And because of that—oh how I've been blessed by your caring!"

"Well, you've always been very self-sufficient and capable—a take charge sort of person—but I've noticed the change in you lately, in letting go a little, in *leaning*, as you put it. Bonnie, I don't think I've ever felt closer to you than I do right now."

"I feel just the same way. . . . It's weird, but I'm glad I got to experience a new way of being, Mom. Guess that's another benefit of these exotic medications, so to speak. And if—"

Just then the phone rang an interruption.

150

151

"I'll get it, dear." Murra hurried to answer and came back from the kitchen with the cordless unit. "For you, from work. Do you feel up to it?"

"I'll be fine." Bonnie reached for the phone. "Yes? Hi Ellen. The McCormack account?" Smiling, "Yes, it's in the stack on top of the filing cabinets labeled 'Hold for Company to Get its Act Together, aka Nag These at the Beginning of Every Week.' The phone nag numbers are on sticky notes on the top sheets. . . . And you need to know if Medicare covers *what* medication? Whew, that's a wild one—must be so new nobody's ever heard of it. I can say confidently that Medicare doesn't, at least not yet. . . . Oh heavens, it's no problem calling me at home; let me know if there's anything else I can do. . . . Well, thank you so very much!—your thoughts and prayers are what keep me going. . . . Okay Ellen, later. Bye bye."

Murra took the phone from her and set it on the coffee table. "They need you!"

"They're doing a lot better than they give themselves credit for. They'll be okay pretty soon."

Bonnie settled back in position for a head rub, possibly one of the most exquisite parts of her mother's therapy. After a few minutes of such bliss that the deep aching seemed to fade briefly away, she murmured, "I think we need to go to Hawaii again."

Slightly startled, "Are you feeling well enough for that?"

"Hmmm. I don't feel fabulous; but since I have to be *somewhere* during these weeks, I may

152

as well be in the place I love most. I mean, if I got horribly sick, I could hurry up and come home; but I'd like to spend a little while there one last time (if that turns out to be the case). Would *you* be up for it, arthritis and all?"

"Oh, you bet! It would be tremendous, but I don't want you to do anything that will make life harder than it already is."

"I'd like to ask Angelina to come along and a few old friends from Canada and around the country that I haven't seen for years."

"How long would you want to be gone?"

"I was thinking of renting an condo for a week or two, say on Maui where the pace is slow and easy, balmy and mild. I could start making all the reservations now—the internet makes it almost instantaneous. And it'll give me something to occupy my mind—you know, a purpose!"

"If you take all the preparations slow."

Smiling, "Moth-er!"

"Just trying to help!

"How about if I make one call, rest for awhile, make another call, rest for an additional while, make another call—you get the idea."

With a short laugh, "I like the parts that involve resting a whole lot; they're my favorite."

"But when it's all said and done, Mom, I hope you'll like the parts about Maui better than anything."

"Angelina, it's so great of you to drive us into LA!" Bonnie exclaimed as she and her mother settled into their friend's SUV that they would be leaving in long-term parking at LAX.

She looked at Bonnie over the top of her sun glasses with a deadpan expression saying, *"Duh! You're giving me a wonderful week in Hawaii!—jeez, are you kidding? This is the least I could do!"* What she actually did say was less teasing, "It's my pleasure, doll."

The several hour journey through the desert, through the city of Riverside, and then through the eastern communities of Los Angeles along the foothills of the San Gabriel Range swished by quickly, for everyone was in a festive mood, full of anticipation.

"How are you going to feel dealing with a five hour flight?" Angelina asked as at last they swung into the Santa Monica freeway from the Pomona across the endless sprawl of the LA basin.

"Triumphant!" Bonnie laughed.

"Well, tootsie, I knew *that!* But how will you *deal* with it?"

"With the utmost fatigue, no doubt."

Murra couldn't help her concern, "Are you sure you really want to do this, Bonnie?"

"Of course. I'll be sitting down. I'd be sitting down at home just the same way. No sweat."

Before long they turned onto Lincoln Boulevard leading in the most direct way from this last freeway to the airport. Hamburger stands and supermarkets, strip malls and liquor stores, all with a riot of competing signs erupting into visual chaos, filled these next minutes. The faint tang of salt in the air said Venice Beach and the posh marina were near. And at the top of the bluff sat Playa del Rey and the Los Angeles In-

154

ternational Airport.

"Eee-haw!" Bonnie cheered.

"Oh baby!" Angelina echoed with a laugh.

The flight over the Pacific, as ever, involved a great deal of sitting still and trying to read or sleep while limitless blue sea spread below. Finally, the plane landed at the Kahului Airport on Maui.

"I'll go get the rental car," said Bonnie, "while you two take care of the luggage. How does that sound?"

"Maybe I should get the car," Angelina suggested.

"I can walk more easily than I can lift all our dozens of pairs of shoes stuffed in those suitcases—if you're trying to make life easier for me, old friend."

"Okay. Gotcha."

The rental desk turned out to be farther than Bonnie had expected, and by the time she had joined the others—by pulling up to the curb in a nice white van—her bones felt like they were on fire. Even still, once the bags were loaded into the back, she insisted on doing the driving to the rented condo herself.

"I have the directions in mind, guys. It'll be easier if I just go ahead and get us there."

"But Bonnie—" Murra began.

"No buts; I'm doin' it!"

The two climbed inside with no more words. They understood that Bonnie needed to feel capable and in control of the life she felt slipping away, and they were willing to humor her. Still, that didn't stop Angelina from pleating her forehead with concern or Murra from praying for safety from accidents and wrong turns.

As it happened, the condo at Kaanapali Beach on the western end of the island was a little hard to find because of winding roads and fewer than profuse numbers of signs. Still, at last they managed to arrive.

"Whew," said Bonnie with an undeniably flat tone. Fatigue and pain shouted from every inch of her body.

"Yeah, ditto," sighed Angelina. "Where are we supposed to be?—on the second floor?—As you said, 'whew.'"

Murra verified the location with a not necessarily joyful expression. "Think we can make it up there with all this luggage?"

"Let's check it out."

Everyone climbed out and scooped up whatever bags were light and handy without unpacking the van just yet. The air was balmy and sumptuous with a hint of a breeze, but the three hardly noticed it for their focus on getting up to the apartment and having their weary selves, especially Bonnie, settled.

"Gads," Angelina laughed as they finally sweated up to the door. "I hope the beds in here have Magic Fingers because we've *truly* earned some physical pampering!"

"I'll be fine with a Jacuzzi," said Bonnie, "or maybe just straight lying down flat forevermore."

"What about our imperative appreciation of the gorgeous view?"

"You can pull open the drapes so I can

156

see outside from my pillow!"

"As I said, gads." Angelina swiped the key card, and the door unlocked. "Bravo—we're home!"

The three crossed into the apartment and set their gear on the long kitchen counter extending half way down the left hand wall.

"Oh my, this is lovely," Murra exclaimed. "Just look at that view there! We're right on the beach!" She walked to the far end of the long room and opened the glass door out onto the balcony. Off to the left the legendary Black Rock of Kaanapali jutted out massively into the deep crystalline blue of the ocean, and palm trees swayed a lazy tempo against the scene. "Come here, Bonnie—you just have to see this before you lie down."

Both Bonnie and Angelina had joined her on the balcony. Now everybody noticed the restful breeze enfolding the tropical loveliness, the way it lifted their hair and mouthed kisses at their skin.

"They don't call this paradise for nothin'," Bonnie quipped. "Nap time!"

"So much for paradise!"

"I'll get to see it later after I finish sacking out. Meanwhile, you two can fetch the luggage!"

"Thanks a ton, hon."

"My pleasure." Smiling, Bonnie moved to one of the bedrooms to take off her clothes and lie down. In effect, she collapsed.

"So, Murra—" Angelina began with a laugh, "are we enough like beasts of burden to manage this baggage transport business?"

"I'm not actually sure, to be honest. But

we'll have to give it a try."

Seven large and medium suitcases and a good deal of time later, the exertion was over; and the two had a chance to rest and take stock. They had both gotten a soda from the machine in the stair well, so they took these out on the balcony to sit down.

"Appears Bonnie's really out cold," Angelina observed. "I'm sure glad she didn't insist on helping with all that heavy stuff."

"I hear you. It's hard for her to feel like she's not pulling her weight, but I'm thankful she went right in to rest."

"So what's next? I think you said something about Bonnie's friend Elaine from New Jersey flying in this evening?"

"Yes, her flight is due to arrive around 6:30, so I guess we should figure on seeing her some time after 8:00."

"Should we both just veg out until she gets here? Nap, shower, or something requiring zero effort? I'm really pooped."

"That sounds perfect to me, dear."

And so the late afternoon and some of the evening drowsed by.

The clock said it was nearly 9:00.

Bonnie had wakened a little before that and was just finishing a hot bath and a change into airy clean clothes to be ready for her old friend's arrival. But where was she?

"I just realized that we're going to need some groceries," Murra said. "Wish I'd thought of it earlier so we'd have it done before Elaine gets here."

158

"Oh, listen—" Angelina spouted, "I can run down to the grocery store right now while you two are waiting. It'll just take me a second."

"Why don't we all go when she gets here—she's bound to be arriving any minute."

"Okay, if you're sure."

Bonnie was now coming out of the bathroom; and just as she did, a knock at the door suggested the waiting for Elaine was over.

Opening the door widely, Bonnie's eyes were filled. "Elaine! How completely incredible to see you! And all in one piece after so many endless flights! How are you, kiddo?"

"Bonnie, Bonnie! This is just the most fantastic treat. Flights, smights! Anything it took to get here was worth seeing your beautiful face again. You look fabulous!"

"Well, thank you, sweet one—so do you! Come in and get comfy. Elaine, you remember my mother, Murra? And this is my friend Angelina who lives near me these days."

The greetings were hearty all around; the air was thick with celebration. But after a short time of sitting down and exclaiming over the details of their trip with one another, the subject of the grocery store arose once again.

"We'll all go, and I'll drive," said Elaine. "Except maybe you could stay here and guard the house, Bonnie?"

"What am I?—Pouffie your pet poodle?"

"Pouffie is my dearest friend in the whole world, darling," she said with a straight face. "That's a compliment!"

"Do you still have Pouffie?"

"Nope, sorry—it's Homer the gigantic St.

Bernard. And when he guards the house, he really *guards* it."

Murra and Angelina, admittedly, were a bit lost during this exchange; but the spirits were so high, strict attention to meaning didn't seem all that important.

"Maybe you could have some crackers and 7-Up to tide you over, Bonnie," said Murra when she saw a sort of opening in the nonsense.

"That would be super, Mom. Thanks for thinking of it."

The three got ready to leave, and soon the grocery (and wine on sale) trip was complete. They trooped up the two flights of stairs at the condo once more, discussing the fastest thing they could whip up for dinner. When they got inside, though, they found Bonnie fast asleep from the extraordinarily long day, so they snacked and sipped and chatted until they were ready to head off to bed as well.

The new day found everyone rested and Bonnie feeling far more energetic than the rough traveling day before. After a number of hours of lounging on the balcony, catching up on old times and sharing current news, the four decided an exceptional meal would be all that remained for perfection to be achieved.

"There appears to be a wonderful-sounding rib place not far from here," Murra suggested as the one in charge of touring the yellow pages for restaurants. "And they appear to have exotic drinks."

"The kind with little umbrellas or ceramic/feathered parrots on sticks?" Angelina

160

joined her in reading the ad.

"I can't be sure, but I'll bet they have things just as cute."

"Sold!" Bonnie piped. "That sounds perfect, Mom."

Everyone hurried to get ready, and before long they were settling into a table at the rib specialty place overlooking the apparently infinite beach. Sugary white sand stretched into limitless aquamarine with sail boats drifting lazily in front of the horizon. And lovely Hawaiian music floated on the air, wrapping the guests in a subtle rhapsody of sound.

"I can't believe we're really here, Bonnie!" Elaine said with a smile. "This is like a dream, something outside of reality."

"Yes. Can you imagine *living* here full time? A permanent vacation. I think if I had it to do over, I'd start out my career and strive to do my living *here* instead of—wherever else."

"I'd second that," Angelina added. "What were we thinking to have settled for other parts of the world?"

Murra patted her daughter's hand. "Well, at least you had the good sense to bring us here now, and it really *is* a dreamland."

After the fancy drinks cooling under their tropical umbrellas and the enormous sandwiches (which were too much for anyone's lunch-time stomach and needed to be swept home for everyone's doggy), the little group decided to stroll around the nearby shops.

Inside the Dandelion Bookseller they found calendars and the necessary postcards every trip claims as its due.

161

"Do you think we'll get these written before the return flight home?" Elaine said with a wink at Bonnie as she paid for her items. "Is it just me, or do any of you have trouble taking the time to get them done? I'd hate for mine to end up with a New Jersey postmark."

"It's everybody's problem, 'Lainie—too involved in feeling the intoxicating stupor of paradise. It's documented how it wipes out the brain cells."

"Well, Bring It On!"

They sauntered along a short boardwalk edging some upscale gift and specialty boutiques. One in particular caught their interest.

"Oh gads," blurted Angelina, "check this out! 'She Shells'—what a cute name for a dress shop."

"How sweet." Bonnie was drawn close to the window. "And I love that adorable yellow dress on display there. Summery! What are those raised white shapes printed on there?"

"Looks like crusty starfish, sort of abstract," Murra declared. "The pale yellow would look lovely on you, Bonnie."

"Well, I do believe I need to get that dress, folks!"

The group entered the shop laughing, three to browse, one to try on the dress slipped off the mannequin.

In a few minutes, once Bonnie had apparently pulled on the outfit back in one of the fitting rooms, a particular sound caused everyone in the store to pause and then chuckle. "Eeee-haw!" filled the air; it could only have been Bonnie.

162

"I guess that's a yes on the dress," Angelina laughed.

As the appropriate credit card made its way to the clerk's hands, Bonnie stood still there at the checkout desk with a faraway expression in her eyes.

"What is it, dear?" Murra breathed beside her.

"I don't want to be a wet blanket on the fun here," she replied confidentially, "but I have an intension for this dress—that is, an occasion when I want to be wearing it."

Her mother's skin blanched to the color of chalk. "Oh. You mean—uh, burial?" She cleared her throat. "Okay. When the time comes, I'll remember, and you'll be wearing it." Murra walked away to conceal the tears that had started burning her eyes. *"She doesn't even look sick; how can the worst be happening?"* she reflected. *"God, we need a miracle. I just can't let her go."*

Meanwhile, everyone had congregated on the boardwalk once more with ideas and observations.

"Has anyone noticed a jewelry store?" Bonnie asked. "I need to look for a sort of charm to go on a necklace." She didn't explain what purpose such an item would serve, only that it was her intention to find it.

"I saw a place called The Coral Sea about a block back," said Elaine. "The place was mystically dragging me in, but I resisted."

"Well, resist no more! Let's have a look." Bonnie patted her friend on the shoulder, and the four turned around to retrace their steps.

Once inside, they found the shop to be

strictly upper crust, with jewels glinting from every corner. Bonnie headed straight for a section that seemed to offer the sort of charms she was looking for.

"I'll just be a minute," she said.

"Oh, don't hurry—there's plenty here for us to drool over."

Bonnie surveyed the collection with high attention. *"I need something symbolic, something as a remembrance. . . ."* Almost as if magnetically drawn, her gaze fell on a tiny golden sandal with a small ruby set where the straps crisscrossed over the toe. "This is incredible, exactly what I had in mind. No need to keep looking; this is perfect. Now if I can have the back engraved—let's see."

She approached the sales associate and asked her questions. Finding that engraving was indeed an option, she said, "I'd like nine of these little sandals, each with the inscription, 'For the footsteps of our lives. Love, Bonnie, 2003.' Do you think you can get all that on the back without the words' being microscopic?"

"Oh, sure, no problem. We do this sort of miniature work all the time."

"Super. So you have a team of elves, do you?"

"How did you know!"

"Psychic, I guess. But listen, I also need nine gold necklace chains, one to go with each of the charms. Each will need a separate gift box, and you can send the whole works to this address—" Bonnie scribbled her home address on one of the shop's business cards and handed it, along with her credit card, to the clerk.

164

"Would you like to pick out the particular chain?"

"Yes, . . . how about this simple, straightforward one?" Bonnie replied, pointing downward in the display case. "That one looks perfect: plain enough not to detract from the charm itself."

"Will that be all for you today?"

"Yes, thank you. These are very special and important to me, and I want to thank you for being part of the process." Once the transaction was complete, she moved off with the reflection, *"One of these necklaces for each of my dear girls at work and one for Mom—to remember. Hope I can keep from getting choked up just thinking about it. . . . Snap out of it, kiddo."* Quite casually she wandered over toward the diamonds where her group was remarking on which of them would fulfill their ultimate dreams. "Communing with Girls' Best Friends, are we, ladies?" she said with a laugh.

Angelina had tried on a six carat rock and was holding it up to catch the light. "Oh baby! This one will do fine!"

"Okay, so when you finish paying for it—I hate to bring this up, but—would you mind if I go back to the condo to lie down? You all can certainly feel free to keep shopping till you're drooping, but I think I'm going to need some rest before Connie gets here this evening."

They were all aware of another of Bonnie's friends joining them today, and the four hurried to take care of getting Bonnie to bed. With this reminder of her health, abruptly the deepest reason they all were in this place and at this time hit them with the force reality often has of throwing down the sweetest moment to the bottom. Subdued, they walked back to the restaurant where the van was parked and soon had made their way back to the condo.

"Everybody be happy and sight-see or something!" Bonnie declared as they made their way up the two flights of stairs. "Please—don't pay any attention to me and my dopey naps, okay? I'll feel bad if you hang around here doing nothing while paradise is beckoning just on the other side of these walls."

Once she had persuaded them that she was fine with remaining behind, Bonnie settled into the most infinite feather down of her life and sighed with contentment. Just outside beyond the balcony, the plash of Pacific waves lulled her into a state of peace beyond herself; and she felt that, one way or another, everything was going to be all right.

Connie's various connecting flights from Colorado Springs to Maui managed to get her to the island at the scheduled time, and her trip out to the beach occurred right after that. The little group of guests had gone out for sight-seeing adventures; but Bonnie was awake and ready to receive her old friend, a former co-worker from far in the past.

Few afternoons had held such a high degree of laughter and reminiscence as this one, and the two rekindled their close relationship over several hours on the balcony as if no years had intervened since the last time they were together.

"Do you remember the time we were watching out the office windows down to the parking lot and that gal from the office down the hall apparently had forgotten her car keys?" Connie was saying. "What was her name?"

"Liz. I think it was Liz."

"Yes! Amazing how you remembered that. Anyway, how she tried everything to get into her car and finally figured out a way to open the moon roof so she could climb in—high heels, tight skirt, and all—from above?"

Bonnie smiled. "Resourceful. She was a kind of Hero of the Practical to us ever after that."

"Yes, but remember how comical it seemed at the time? . . . What an odd memory. I wonder why I thought of it?"

"Laughing in the face of hardship to lighten the load?"

Abruptly solemn, Connie gazed straight into Bonnie's eyes. "You mean like we're doing right now?"

Bonnie's expression fell. "Oh, that. Yeah, let's not talk about it, Con, okay?"

Smiling, she said softly, "Okay. You never did like to deal with negatives, my friend, did you? How can you possibly be managing right now?"

With a strict measure, "By not going there. Period."

The words fell heavily, and then Connie regrouped. "Gotcha. I'm sorry for—"

"No, it's okay. But it's better not to dwell on the unthinkable; all it does is spoil the short time we have."

167

Connie nodded. "Okay, but be advised that there are all kinds of things I want to say to you that I'm—"

"—going to leave unsaid while we continue laughing about the good old days. Right?"

"Yes, right." Connie gaze lifted to the breaker line of the beach, and she breathed in the glory of the air's salty tang. "You really knew what you were doing when you chose this place to meet."

"It's just the best, isn't it? If we could bottle the essence of Maui and hand it out at everybody's birth, just think what a great world we'd have."

"No question about it. Amen."

The two continued their happy talk until the others returned from their exploring. At that point, since nearly everyone was ready for dinner, the entire group decided on a seafood place while Bonnie opted out for her bedroom.

"Sorry guys, but I need to lie down. I really don't mind staying behind; I just want to be sure you all have a grand time while you're here. Go have some exotic drinkie-poos and the most decadent shrimp you can find. I'm counting on you for my vicarious thrills! Go for it!"

"I'll stay here to rub your back, Bonnie," Murra said at once. "I still have my doggy bag from lunch if I get hungry later on."

"You don't need to do that, Mom."

"It's my biggest pleasure, dear."

The next day two more of Bonnie's friends arrived, Kerrie and Gennine who were both living in the Milwaukee area. Without delay, the chat-

168

ter of six women confined in the condo started to raise the roof, so the group—including Bonnie this time, so long as she was away from her bed no longer than three hours—decided to take it outside. They chose the patio of an Italian joint along the beach for a hearty lunch.

Gennine insisted on three bottles of champagne and toasts to cover everything from old (as well as newly formed) friendships to wishes that Bonnie's health go back into remission. The voices around the table accumulated additional volume with the festive fizz of the wine. And when the eight-layered lasagna arrived with an exceedingly attentive server, the high spirits covering their sense of tragedy rose even more.

"I was expecting a layer of pineapple in here with the garlic and mozzarella cheese," Angelina buzzed at once. "Didn't know Hawaiian chefs felt comfortable making dishes without that in them."

"And cocoanut!" Bonnie cried.

"That too!"

After the meal, everyone decided window shopping would be a good way to work off all the bulk they had consumed.

Murra watched as Bonnie agreed to go along. *"I'm so afraid she might collapse,"* she told herself. *"But I dare not say anything that would challenge her sense of control. What's a mother to do? An age old question!"*

They all set out among a short cluster of shops, exclaiming at the local color featured in the gifts and wares.

A widely grinning native fellow in a Hawaiian shirt focusing red and riotous rose hues was sitting in front of one of these playing a ukulele. The effect seemed magnetic, and the little group was drawn into the store behind him, Aumakua Books and Prints. The shop, named for the spirits of the ancestors, welcomed them with warm greetings and a flower for everybody's hair.

After they all had time to browse, Elaine decided she could not face future life in New Jersey without a CD exploring tropical rain forest sounds. And Murra found a wonderful watercolor print of the palm-swept Maui shoreline with rhapsodic clouds and rippling sea surmounted by the most tranquil of rainbows; the scene held a promise of joy amid the storms of life that seemed somehow symbolic of the quintessential Bonnie. Realizing that, she hesitated not one second to buy it for Bonnie's living room wall back home.

She glanced at her daughter on the way out of the shop and murmured, "How are you holding up? Would you like me to go back to the condo with you?"

Bonnie sighed. "Yes, but I wish I could say no. Would you mind? I think I've really overextended myself this time, Mom."

"I don't mind in the least."

Once Bonnie had reiterated that she wanted her guests to continue having the best of times while she hurried back to rest, they all set out for more shopping while the two made their way back to the condo on the beach.

Two days later Elaine was due to fly back to New Jersey. For the occasion, Bonnie and Murra had

170

ordered a gift from a local florist as a send off.

"What on earth?" Elaine burst when the box was placed in her hands. "Oh you two!" Inside she found an exquisite orchid lei in shades of pastel pink to wear on the way home. She settled it around her neck with tears in her eyes. And the hug she had for her old friend was all-encompassing, believing it would be the last time. "Bonnie, my dear sweet Bonnie. . . . Thank you for this and for the time here in Hawaii! But how can I say all the other things running through my mind? I know you don't want me to make a scene, but—good grief, I love you! I'll always remember what a beautiful friend you've been to me."

"And you have been to me, Elaine. Forever."

Their eyes met and soaked in decades of time in the looking. "I'm trying not to cry, Bonnie."

Smiling radiantly, "So am I!"

After a pause, "Guess I'd better scoot." And after they stood still for some pictures, Elaine was gone.

During that same afternoon, another of Bonnie's friends, Sharon, a supervisor at the Cancer Foundation of the Desert where Bonnie worked, flew in from LAX and drove over from the Kahului airport. She was a woman who felt deep love and admiration for her afflicted co-worker and friend, and her single focus in coming here to Maui was to see Bonnie, never mind the tropical sights of paradise.

Although Bonnie had been feeling on the

edge of collapse most of the time during these two weeks, this afternoon her strength took a turn for the better. Out on the balcony of the condo, vitally in savoring distance of the plash of water along the beach, the group took seats with iced tea and spent some time together, talking and laughing—at times uproariously. Bonnie had always been a vivid storyteller, and today she had the energy to treat her friends to some tales of earlier times.

"Oh, I remember a day when my friend Leslie and I were at the Santa Monica beach. We thought we were pretty hot stuff and decided we'd see if we could persuade the fellow at the refreshment stand at the pier to sell us some beer—that is, we were hoping to pass for twenty-one."

"How old were you actually?" Sharon asked.

"We weren't a hair over eighteen."

"So how did it turn out?"

"Well, we stood around acting what we thought was excessively *mature*, but we never did get up the nerve to pop the question to the guy behind the counter. After awhile, we sort of shrugged it off and started wandering along, checking out the merry-go-round and exhibits along the pier. We saw a lot of old guys fishing and plenty of fathers with little boys doing that as well; but all of a sudden we noticed two men following us. Certainly we took off running like any innocent person will automatically do, but they caught up with us."

"Gads, were you in trouble about something?" Angelina piped in. "You can't get arrested

172

for just *looking like* you wanted to buy beer!"

"No, but they asked how old we were and made us show our IDs and stuff. As it turned out, they were looking for two runaway *fourteen* year old girls and thought we might be those two." Laughing with complete joy, "And here we thought we were such hot chicks that we could pass for twenty-one!"

The group chuckled at the sweetness of the story, and then Bonnie went on with high spirits.

"Another time, years earlier, I had gotten in trouble for—"

"I didn't know you ever got in trouble, Bonnie," Sharon teased.

Glancing at her mother with a grin, "Yeah, sometimes—ask Mom! But this particular time I was sent to bed without my dinner. Picture this, if you will—my brother, taking pity on me as a poor, pathetic waif, lowered some dinner to me on a rope out his window. Imagine this sloppy Joe hamburger stuff dangling in front of my eyes beyond the curtains in my room; it sounds like something out of 'Leave it to Beaver,' doesn't it?"

The mood was wonderful in the group, and everybody laughed at the scene. Most of the other stories continued to center on childhood and adolescent silliness, the sort of thing that makes our lives rich and colorful; but this last story came from only several months before and involved one of her "girls" at work, Kristin Bennet, the artist.

"Now this is going to end up being a slice of slapstick, folks," Bonnie was saying, "and might not translate as funny if—"

173

"—if you weren't there, right?" Angelina said, finishing the thought.

"Exactly. This happened one afternoon after many (though not all) people had gone home for the day but while it was still light outside. Kristin was on her way out the door but stopped in my office for a little chat while I was still finishing up the day's insurance claims. Here's the scene:

"Just wanted to wish you a happy evening, Bonnie. How are you feeling after such a long day as this was?"

"Pretty wonderful, actually."

With just a hint of a frown, hoping for something a little closer to the truth than my body language must've been proclaiming, "Are you sure? You seem a little down; heaven knows, you have a right to be."

"Even when I just said I'm up?"

Softly, "Yes, even then."

I could only smile, "Are you eyeballing my insides and saying my outside doesn't match?—something like wearing one red sock along with one purple one?"

"Sort of. Is there anything I can help you with?"

"No, sweet one, but thank you for asking."

"Well, goodnight, then,"

"Good night."

Kristin bopped in and out of a few offices down the hall (keep in mind that most of the walls are made of see-through-able glass), saying good night to anyone else she happened to see. Then she headed out of the building into the flower bower-y courtyard outside my office.

174

She gave a final hearty wave with her whole arm. I waved in return, but the gesture must've appeared to be waving her back into the building, as if I had something else to say.

Immediately Kristin turned toward my office, wholly intent on finding out what I wanted to tell her. The only thing she forgot was to open the door to the building; and instead, she slammed directly into my office window. With a loud whomping thud, Kristin landed on the ground in the chrysanthemums. Dazed, she glanced up and saw me running out of my office and into the hallway doubled over.

When Kristin had gathered her senses and wandered back into the building, she found several people who had rushed out to console me (in their midst). Surely I looked like I needed such consolation: why else would I be charging through the hall shrieking hysterically "Bird! Bird! Dodo bird!" It must've seemed perfectly and unabashedly insane.

But when they noticed the goose egg popping from Kristin's forehead, they connected the dots and realized I was *laughing*, not crying. And after the whole scene was explained, everyone laughed and joked and carried on—making fun of life, telling stories, and joking as if nothing could ever be so wrong that it could destroy our sense of humor.

"It's the point you always try to make, Bonnie," said Murra. "A sort of theme; we keep coming back to that idea."

"Well, Mom, I feel it with all my heart. And I'm hoping all of you will think of this when . . .

that is, *if* . . . things don't go well for me in the health category . . . so to speak. I guess you know what I mean."

The next day arrived, and it was time for Kerrie and Gennine to return to their homes in Minnesota. They thanked Bonnie for the exhilarating island adventure but, most of all, for sharing some of (possibly) her last days with them.

"You just don't look sick, Bonnie," said Gennine. "It's almost impossible to believe you are."

"I feel exactly the same way," Kerrie echoed.

"That's a *good* thing, isn't it? You can remember me like this, not as someone moaning in a hospital room. Okay?"

The two received elegant flower leis and stood for pictures for everyone to remember. And after more heartfelt talk, they were gone.

Although the two weeks in Maui were drawing to a close, still one more old friend, Nora from Los Angeles, joined them for a last visit with Bonnie. It had been months rather than years— as with most of the other guests—since they had seen one another.

"I'm simply thunderstruck with the beauty of Hawaii, Bonnie. Now I understand why you love to come here so often."

"Amazing, isn't it?" Bonnie replied at the end of their greeting hug.

"Thank you so terrifically for asking me to be with you here."

"Oh, listen—I was glad you could get away

176

for a day or two even if your messy schedule couldn't let it be any longer."

Angelina stepped forward. "You're here just in time for lunch, Nora. Shall we all head out?"

Bonnie shook her head. "I'm afraid I can't do anything but sit and lie down today, Ange; but I'd love it if you'd all would find a lovely place on the beach—something balmy and scrumptious with island fare."

Most of the guests had done this before— found a restaurant even while Bonnie needed to stay back in bed—but one among them, Sharon, said at once, "I'll stay here with Bonnie, and you guys go ahead.

After a little discussion, this is exactly how a small part of the afternoon went. When the others had left for a short lunch, Sharon confided to her beloved friend, "I hope I didn't put anybody off, but I feel like I can see Hawaii on my own any old time. I came here to be with *you*, Bonnie, since we have so little time. Am I being too bossy?"

Smiling, "Of course not, Sharon. You make me feel wonderful to know that's how you see things. . . . Have you been able to observe how my staff is getting along at work without me?"

"They're coming along, but I'd be less than honest if I said the department is cooking on all burners."

"Eeek. That drives me nuts."

"I know it does—you always want everything to be mixed, baked and frosted before you leave in the evening. It makes sense that you'd feel uncomfortable if the cake currently is flopping a bit. It's just going to take a little time."

"As I said, eeek."

"We all miss you more than you could know."

The conversation turned to more personal concerns, and before long the others had returned from lunch. Now the group decided to spend the rest of the day lolling on the beach directly out from the condo, a proposition unmatchable for feeding joy to the spirit as it offered sand and pink shells, breakers echoing through paradise and a majesty of open sky. And so it went.

Now it was the last day. Bonnie, Murra, Angelina, Sharon, and Nora would be taking a night flight to Los Angeles, while Connie was heading out for Colorado Springs this afternoon. The weight of believing it might be the last time they would see Bonnie dragged heavily on all of them.

Connie received her lei with tears forming in her eyes, but she managed not to cry rather well.

"This is hard, Bonnie."

"Yes, believe me, I know."

"I love you; I'll never in this life forget you."

"I love you, too."

This friend gave her a last hug before going to her rental car; but it wasn't enough, and she came back for another one.

"Hang it all! Goodbyes are impossible!"

Chapter Thirteen

December, 2003

This was not the tropical grandeur of paradise; but in being home itself, all the comforts needed for peacefulness were present. Still, though Bonnie was bone tired and feeling quite ill in every imaginable way, she insisted on going to the office immediately after their return.

"What on earth are you doing here!" Beth, her assistant, exclaimed at once. "How long were you home—ten minutes?—before you rushed over here? . . . Gee, it's great to see you! Gotta get a hug!"

Bonnie laughed with happiness. "Just wanted to make sure things are moving along. Mostly I'm here to answer any questions that have been coming up."

Smiling slyly, "How long can you stay? A week? Maybe two?"

"That bad?"

"No, I'm kidding. But I'm sure everyone has a few for you. What's the band-aid for?" she said, nodding toward Bonnie's wrist.

"Oh, I just had a little intravenous treatment with Dr. Menier upstairs."

"Are you feeling okay? I'm almost afraid to ask."

"No, it's fine if you do. I'm just pretty tired from the traveling is all. I'm only here for half the day." Of course, she said nothing about how

178

she really felt.

Bonnie had been wanting to have a get-together for the eight members of her staff, a time to give them the little sandal charm necklaces from Hawaii and reaffirm all their bonds; this seemed like a perfect time to start deciding things. Yet just as she was forming the first sentence of the invitation, the phone rang; and Beth left the office so Bonnie could talk.

The second half day at work was just as busy. The questions from her staff filled the hours, but Bonnie felt satisfied at the end that these dear friends were on their way to having the office under control well enough to get by during this difficult time. Still, the party remained unplanned, and the ache of her head and deep in the bones fell ever more heavily.

"Mom, I'm home!" She set down her purse and keys after work with an air of intense fatigue.

"How did you hold up all those hours?"

"I'm glad I went in to the office, and I plan to try to keep going each morning; but all I can think about is a hot Epsom salts bath and the area under that goose down."

"How do you feel?"

"T-I-R-E-D and about as weak as a cornflake."

"How about if I fix you a little something for dinner?"

Bonnie started to dodge the question out of habit, but then she changed her mind. "Mom, I'm afraid my stomach is a real mess. It feels like there's a brick in there: I can't eat, and I can't go." Softly, "I almost don't know what to do."

Murra stood in the doorway with her hands folded in front of her. "Ahh," she said with a moan. "Oh, Bonnie, I wish I could make it all go away. What can I do to help?"

"It seems weird that after managing to drive home, I would need help getting a bath ready; but I'm afraid it's come down to that. Would you mind?"

"Of course not. You just let me know whatever you need."

About a week later, her cousin Cindie from Canada, one who had been to Hawaii on an earlier trip, announced that she had to visit one last time. She was stricken by the realities surrounding her dear cousin and needed to be with her. And so she arrived.

"It appears that I can't do much but lie here once I'm home from work, sweet one," Bonnie explained.

"That doesn't matter to me in the least; I just wanted to see you."

"Well, I'll tell you what," Murra said while the three occupied the living room, "maybe Cindie and I can go through things, Bonnie, and you can decide what to throw out, what to set aside for which person, all that sort of thing."

"That's a fantastic idea, Mom—honestly. I'm glad you thought of it. But, guys, is it okay if I can't lift my head up with any real enthusiasm?"

Cindie smiled. "It's perfectly okay. How about another pillow to raise you just a tad so you can see what we're holding up in front of you without straining your neck around in weird directions?"

"Sounds good to me."

The week wandered by with Bonnie, her mother, and cousin Cindie determining the fate of her various items—clothing, papers, art objects, Christmas decorations, jewelry—in the evening while she went to work in the morning and slept through long naps in between.

Before long Cindie was due to return home.

"How am I going to say goodbye to you without crying, Bonnie? This is asking too much of a poor human mortal person."

"I know, Cindie, but if we manage to be strong, you'll look back on this time with less pain than if you give into a breakdown."

"I'm not sure that's true; but in any case, my sweet love, I guess all I can say is . . . be safe and God speed."

"I love you."

"I love you, too, Bonnie."

"Mom, I'm home!" As ever, Bonnie set down her keys and purse, but this time she all but dropped them beneath the Christmas wreath just to the side of the door. "Mom?"

"I'm here." Murra came from the kitchen wiping her hands on a towel. "What is it, Bonnie? You look upset."

"Why don't we sit down." They went to the living room just off the entry hall and found seats on the sofa. "I can hardly say this out loud, Mom, but I found myself making mistakes on the accounts this morning. Mistakes! Being at work has been a great distraction, but now this!

Mistakes! I just can't think straight. It's as if the tumors have taken over my brain."

"And is it your eyes as well?"

"No question. . . . This scares me; I've been able to cover up my pain from people pretty well all along, at least up to this time; but mistakes are something else—something out there flapping in the breeze that can affect people's lives. I don't even know what to say except that I don't know if I should risk going to the office any more and messing things up."

"You need to do what's best for you, Bonnie."

"Well, I guess what's best for me in this case will be best for business—if I stay home and don't deal with work any more."

"I would certainly applaud you for following that course. I've always wished you could just rest and build back your strength." Murra laid a hand on her daughter's shoulder. "Would you like a little something to eat?"

Softly, "No, Mom, but thanks. I'm afraid I haven't been able to get any pills down today either. Nothing's going in and nothing's coming out."

"Would you like to take your bath now and just get into bed?"

"That seems like the best I can do."

"I'll get the bed turned down for you."

"Thanks, Mom; that would help a lot."

Bonnie dragged into the bathroom, sprinkled Epsom salts in the tub, and turned on the water.

But then Murra heard a yell—muffled but still unmistakable—and rushed to see what had happened. "Oh my God, Bonnie! What is that?"

Bonnie had thrown up. Yet this was different from the usual in being dark and foul; both believed it was fecal material, and fear jolted through them at a stroke.

"I'll pack a bag for you while you call the doctor, Bonnie. We're going to the hospital—now."

The hospital room was a private one with a vast window offering a view of the mountains rising to the west. The sun set behind them on this mid-December evening with a scarlet bravado, but Bonnie hardly noticed while the staff hooked her up to feeding and drainage tubes and various IV solutions from hanging racks. Her body had essentially shut down from doing these procedures on its own; now she would have the help she needed.

Murra stayed through the night. Her eyes moved uneasily from one vital sign monitor to another; in particular, the jerks of Bonnie's heart rhythms became all but hypnotic as she watched and prayed for signs of normalcy. She noted the wheeze of the blood pressure cuff as it periodically tightened and released.

She fingered the egg-carton mattress provided for Bonnie's profound ache in the bones and added another pair of socks to relieve Bonnie's chilly feet.

During the dark hours while Bonnie slept—thankfully from medication to ease the deep pain she was suffering—Murra marked the number of interruptions of nurses coming and going, checking and re-checking, making notes,

184

and trying to smile with upbeat expressions.

And throughout, Murra's insides felt clenched with a dread that had a name not left to guessing.

The next morning Dr. Menier had a tube put in Bonnie's nose down to her stomach and ordered all manner of injections to aid in her comfort.

"All I can think about is a chocolate milk shake!" Bonnie exclaimed to the morning nurse. "When did you say the dessert cart comes around?"

Smiling, "Shouldn't be too long now. I think I hear it rattling out in the hall."

"Great. The way I figure, a drinking straw (hooked up to a milk shake) is pretty much like any of these other tubes I have dangling here; what's another tube among friends?" Her eyes sparkled merrily.

"Well, there's no question that you have a fine array of them."

Just then the hospital florist entered the room with four artful arrangements, each with a Christmas motif. The white poinsettias with pine and silver tinsel were especially magnificent.

"Are those ever amazing!" Bonnie whooped. "Let me see the cards, Mom!" She tore open the tiny envelopes at once. "These are from my staff as a group at work; the red rose bouquet is from the Cancer Foundation itself as a whole; the pink poinsettias are from brother Gene and Charlene and the kids; and the gold and white one is from brother Ed and Grace. Do I ever feel blessed to have such caring sent my way!"

And out in the hall voices of visitors could be heard in low tones.

"What is there, a line of sweet people out there?" Bonnie laughed.

"Hey, kiddo—what's a gal like you doing in a place like this?" Angelina sputtered upon entering the room.

"Hi Ange. I'm serving as a tube rack at the present time as you can obviously see. Apparently. How great of you to come by!"

"This is the one place I needed to be, tootsie." She paused to set a chubby fabric Santa on the bedside table. "I don't know if you have room for any more Christmas decorations, but I didn't think you could do without Santa Claus listening to your gift selections."

"Well, I have one particular gift in mind— a chocolate milk shake. And I'd like it *now* rather than waiting the thirteen more days till Christmas."

"If Santa can't take care of it, nobody can."

"This little fellow looks mighty powerful." Bonnie took him into her hands and brought him close for a hug and kiss on the nose.

Now Kristin and Beth from work made their way into the room with a deep pink azalea plant.

"Just wanted you to know that we love you, Bonnie," Kristin began.

"Yes, and how sad we are that you're stuck here instead of anywhere else on the planet, especially at work with us." Beth set the azaleas on the ledge of the window with the four other arrangements. "Everybody sends their love and

186

said to tell you they'd be by to see you after work today or during lunch."

"What a mob of fantastic friends I have!"

"But how do you feel, Bonnie?" Kristin asked.

"Like a trussed turkey! How do I look?"

"Like a trussed turkey!"

"Well, eee-haw! Guess the folks here are doin' their jobs!"

These visits were cut short in a little while by a nurse with her patient's well-being in mind. "You can come back later, ladies; but right now Bonnie is scheduled for some tests and then will need to rest." Everyone, including Murra for awhile, said their goodbyes and wandered off into the hall and then to the parking lot.

Before long two nurses from the radiology department stopped by to transport Bonnie for an X-ray. Her eyes scanned the overhead lights in the corridors as the maze of them slipped by. And at last they arrived.

The sheening metal surface of the table cut into her sore body like a row of knives.

"I can't do this," Bonnie murmured with a stricken expression.

"It'll only take a minute," the technician breezed in reply.

"No, I mean I *can't do this!*"

"Hold your breath!" A whirring sound filled the small silence. "Breathe." The tech, skimming along on the surface of tone to hide his guilt of having ignored Bonnie's cry of pain, hurried to get her off the tormenting table. "Sorry about that," he mumbled at last.

Bonnie chose not to comment.

Back in her room, the period of rest was a welcome respite; and Bonnie filled it with dozing for most of the afternoon.

When her eyes opened during this time, she found the faces of Dr. Menier's wife and two daughters around her.

"Pam—how fantastic to see you! What a surprise."

"Brad has been talking about very little else since you were admitted; he's so deeply affected. I'm so very sorry, Bonnie, that you have to be here like this."

The older of the girls smiled and wiggled a pert Christmas tree that she was holding in front of her. "We thought we'd bring some holiday decorations for you since you're stuck here," she said.

"Well, I can't imagine anything nicer. I *do* miss having my tree to look at; my mom had just finished setting it up a few days before I had to come here. Thank you ever so much for thinking of that."

The two girls settled the tree on the ledge closest to Bonnie's head so she could see it easily.

"It's hard to be away from home at this time of year." Even as she said it, Pam realized how inadequate the sentiment must sound under the circumstances. But how close to the truth would be appropriate when spoken aloud?

Just then Murra returned; and almost immediately after that, Angelina popped in as well. Since the room was getting crowded, Pam Menier wished Bonnie well and promised to come back with her two girls tomorrow.

188

"So! How are you doing this afternoon, tootsie?" Angelina began.

"I guess all these tubes are helping because I feel lots better than when I checked in, I'm here to tell ya."

"That's super, no kidding." She fidgeted a bit with the little Santa she had brought earlier. "Listen, kiddo—I have a sort of surprise for you.

"What kind of surprise?"

"I arranged to have Hospice get involved with your care. You should be seeing someone from their outfit any minute now."

Almost as if she had been slapped, Bonnie cried, "Hospice! I don't want to have Hospice! Why did you do that?"

Taken aback slightly by Bonnie's unexpected vehemence, "Because I've always thought they were the best at comforting people when—"

"What? When they're dying?"

"Well, yes."

"But I'm going to kick this thing, Angelina! This isn't the end, so I don't need any people tromping in here and treating me like it is!"

"Gads, tootsie, I'm sorry. I never meant to hurt you. I'm so very sorry. I'll call them up right now and cancel. I'm really sorry." With her mind spinning over the idea of causing her best friend pain, Angelina ducked out of the room to take care of her phone call.

"Why are you looking at me like that, Mom?" Bonnie blurted at once.

"It's just sadness. I'm sorry everything feels so extreme right now; we're all trying so hard to deal with your illness, and sometimes—"

"It's okay," Bonnie said softly, "I'm not upset any more. I know she was just trying to help. My reaction must've seen ridiculously out of character for me."

"Not when you consider how much giving up isn't part of the way you handle life." And, Murra thought to herself, *What will I ever do if I lose my Bonnie?*

"I hope she won't be mad at me."

"No, dear, I don't think she will. She loves you, and she's very frightened." Pausing to switch gears, "Would you like me to read to you—since your eyes are so bad? I brought along a *Newsweek* in case you'd like to be up-to-date on the world's doings."

"That would be fine, Mom. Thank you."

A number of days followed one another with the slow pace and sameness of hospitals everywhere but punctuated by steady streams of visitors and flowers, people whose lives had been specially touched by Bonnie's kindness bearing tokens of their esteem. And among these days, still another morning had risen, one closer still to Christmas. This morning hour was the time Murra would arrive each day and stay until late afternoon.

"Hi, Bonnie—how are you feeling?"

"Great! As ever, the nights are rough, but with the sun today I feel on top of the world. So to speak. I tell you this, of course, from flat on my back."

"Well, your color is better."

"Ridiculously rosy cheeks?"

"Almost."

190

"Listen, Mom. I'd really love it if you could get some of that dry shampoo they have here and see if you could de-grunge my hair. I feel like a barbarian lolling around here with a gooey—though curly!—mop. I want to look nice!"

Smiling, "I think that's a good sign!"

"And maybe I could have a razor blade?"

"Bonnie!"

"No, not to end it all—but for my legs. As I said, I want to look nice."

"Well, you've got it." Murra busied herself to take care of these wishes.

Once she had received some of the special shampoo from the nurses' station, she set about to work it into Bonnie's scalp. "It's nifty stuff, isn't it?"

"Yes, it certainly is. . . . Mom, try not to rub too hard—my head is just so sore that almost any pressure sends little shocks all through me."

"Oh! I'm so sorry."

"No problem, just thought I needed to mention it."

Once all the primping was complete, Bonnie smiled with radiance and said, "Better? Less cruddy?"

"You were fine to begin with!"

"You're biased, Mother Dear."

Just then a man from the mortuary, whom Bonnie had called, knocked on the door and came in.

"You wanted to see me about the particulars, Ms. Kenneford?" he said in a somber tone.

"Yes. I want to pay you, and I want to be sure that the casket will be closed during the funeral—that is, if I'm due to have either of those

. . . guess I will at some point if not right away. Anyway, will you be sure that's taken care of?"

"Of course," he said, writing a note to himself.

"Why is that, dear?" Murra couldn't help but ask. "Your friends would want to say goodbye to you."

"Mom, I don't want anybody staring at me and counting my warts while they admire that yellow starfish dress I got in Hawaii."

"Bonnie, you don't have warts!" But Murra pulled back from the discussion because she did understand that Bonnie's sense of control would be unhinged by her death; she would not want people judging her silent form. Murra stood at the foot of the bed for a few minutes, considering this truth.

Meanwhile, Bonnie had written a check to cover the funeral expenses and was just handing it to the mortuary representative.

"You know this will be my final home," she said to him.

The man appeared shocked at the lightness of her tone. "Yes, ma'am, but excuse me if I observe that you don't look sick at all—well, except for all the tubes and hardware."

Smiling, "That's what everybody says," she replied. "See, Mom? I told you having my hair fresh and legs shaved would do the trick!"

But Murra had walked to the window and was trying to conceal her pounding heart and stricken expression. The contradictions here felt harder than anything she'd ever had to bear.

At last the business was wrapped up in good time.

192

Now Sharon, one of the supervisors at Bonnie's work and one who had visited in Hawaii, entered with a beautiful Christmas wreath of twisted grape twigs with holly and tiny bears. She took one look at her beloved friend lying there, and her eyes started to fill with tears. She moved out into the hall to wipe them and then came back in.

Her smile was wobbling, but Bonnie beamed at her with an inspirational bit of cheer that helped restore her equilibrium.

"You know, Bonnie, I've been reflecting non-stop on a piece of scripture that I wanted to share with you."

"I'd be honored to hear it, Sharon. I'm blessed that you were thinking of me."

"It's from First Corinthians, one of my favorites—the promise that God won't let you carry more of a burden *than you can bear;* you need to know that He won't let you experience a degree of suffering more than you can tolerate. And you can cling to that! Actually, *I'm* clinging to it myself whenever I'm thinking about you. It helps bring peace; maybe thinking about this promise can bring peace to you too."

"I *will* think about it."

Just then a nurse came in to take Bonnie for radiation, so Sharon decided she should leave. "I'll be back to see you, dear Bonnie. You take care. And remember what God promises."

"I will, Sharon. Thank you. And thank you so very much for coming."

The next morning Murra arrived at 7:00 and found nurses bustling about, working toward

Bonnie's comfort, and the doctors making their rounds. The air was chipper, almost festive.

"Hi Mom! Join the party!"

"My goodness—how nice to see you in such good spirits."

"Yes indeed. And I hope I can keep doing my best, that is feeling on top of things as I do this morning."

"That would be first on my list too." After a bit more chat, Murra sat down beside the bed and started reading parts of the paper out loud.

"What's that big ad on the back of the page you're reading? Hamilton's Furniture Holiday Blowout? What does it say?"

Murra turned the paper over and checked out the ad. "Sofas and love seats mostly, Bonnie."

"I've been thinking we should be looking for another sofa for the living room. Maybe rather than the turquoise and rose colors, we should go with something different, say—I don't know—cream leather? Something soft and ridiculously puffy?"

"You're serious?"

"Yes. I've been hanging out on the current one to the point that it's a saggy old bag. Time we spruced up the place."

"It's not saggy!"

"Well, even still, maybe you could look for something new, shop around—that sort of thing."

"Of course I'd be happy to do that." Murra was even more thrilled with the idea of having Bonnie well enough and home to enjoy it. "Yes, it can be a Christmas present to both of us from both of us."

194

"Just getting to go home and sit on it would be present enough for me."

"Amen to that!"

"Speaking of God—"

"Were we?"

"Yes, you know—you said 'Amen'—I'd really like to get hold of Sharon to ask her more about that scripture she told me about yesterday. I had a pretty lonely night, didn't sleep much, and I was thinking about God's promise to not let us carry more of a burden than we can handle. I wanted her to explain that more fully."

"Would you like to try getting her on the phone?"

"That would be great, Mom. Would you mind dialing for me? Her number's in the little book in my purse."

They had no luck reaching Sharon; but Bonnie intended to keep trying, all day if necessary, until she found out what she needed to know.

After awhile, Murra went out in the hall for a drink of water. When she returned, an attendant was there to take Bonnie for another radiation treatment.

"I'm meeting your friend Sarah for lunch, Bonnie, and afterward she wanted to come by to see you. Apparently, she's made one of her cute little items for you."

"What little item exactly?"

"A surprise. She wouldn't tell me, but I'd imagine it's something soft and crocheted. . . . We'll probably be back just about the time you're returning from the treatment."

"It sounds perfect, Mom. Enjoy yourself!"

The hour had passed with Murra and Bonnie in the two separate locations, engaging in the two very different activities. But now, as coincidence would have it, they were meeting in the hall on the way back to Bonnie's room.

"Bonnie! How great to see you!" Sarah exclaimed.

"Hi Sarah. Hi Mom." Bonnie's color had faded from its earlier almost-bloom.

Murra's motherly instincts noticed the change at once, but she said brightly, "How are you feeling? How was the treatment?"

But at that moment Bonnie became deathly pale and her eyes rolled back briefly as if in some agonizing pain.

"Bonnie! What is it!"

In an instant, it seemed that doctors and nurses were running from all directions, a melee of action and motion and purpose. But Murra saw only her daughter's eyes as they now focused on her. And unmistakably the pleading in those eyes said, *"Mom, why do I have to die? I want so much to live. Why, Mom? Why?"*

Surely this is a question murmured by all of humanity, for all of time. And the answer forever remains in the mind of God.

Bonnie had a brain stem hemorrhage there in the hall, a massive and irreversible stroke. And before she could be swept into a treatment room, she slid into a coma.

Before long Murra was joined by Sharon at her vigil in the quiet room.

"I'd like to say goodbye to Bonnie."

An hour, then an hour more passed with Sharon silently stroking Bonnie's arm. The sadness in the room fell heavily and pervaded the very air.

As she was leaving, she gazed into Murra's eyes in the doorway. "Thank you, now I've said my goodbye."

Then Dr. Menier entered the room and remained, sadly meditating, for a short time.

Murra sat quietly reflecting at her daughter's bedside until the end, a serene slipping away as Bonnie went home. The question of why Bonnie was taken so early and in the fullness of a generous, giving life filled her mind. And as she pondered it—and it would be for years—she realized that, though she might not understand the answer in this lifetime, at least Bonnie in the heavenlies understood it now.

Some people come into lives and quickly go.
Some people move our souls to dance;
They awake us to understanding with the courage
of their spirit.
Some people make the sky more beautiful to gaze
upon,
They stay in our lives for a while, leave footprints
on our hearts,
And we are never ever the same.

Author Unknown